GHOSTS

BECKY BRONSON

REBECCA BRONSON, PUBLISHER

Rebecca Bronson, Publisher
Westford, MA USA
www.beckybronson.com

Library of Congress Control Number: 2025914764

First Printing, August 2025
ISBN 978-1-7348551-7-3 (Print)
ISBN 978-1-7348551-6-6 (Ebook)

Cover design by: ebookscoversdesign.com

*G*loomsbury is a nameless city—an amalgam of the countless places in the world where poverty reigns and hatred brews. It is a place of both hopelessness and promise, for if one can understand the root causes of violence here, there may yet be hope for the rest of the world....

1

It started as an ordinary summer day, though for five-year-old Danny and his ten-year-old sister Em, life would never be the same. After spending the morning with Em and her friend Libby at Libby's house down the street, Danny now sat by the tiny window in his dark and gloomy bedroom at home, watching the two girls play hopscotch in his driveway. A single tear fell from his eye as their laughter filtered through the window screen, the sound carried toward him by a hot summer breeze. He wished that heat could penetrate inside him and pierce through the chill of shame and loneliness he felt. When he had tried to join them, Em had snapped at him. "Go away! You're being a pest!" He didn't think he was a pest. He simply wanted to play, but it was clear the girls didn't want him around. Well, that wasn't totally true. Em wanted nothing to do with him, but Libby had smiled shyly at him, as if to say, "*I don't agree.*"

Danny liked Libby because she often persuaded Em to include him. But on this day, Em didn't back down. Through the open window, Danny heard Libby ask his sister why she was so mean to him. "He's a wimp," Em said with a shrug.

Bored and dejected, Danny trudged down the hallway, bristling at the sight of his older brother Sean's locked door. It seemed like no one wanted to play with him. He considered walking away, but knocked quietly, fully expecting Sean to bark at him like Em had. To his surprise, Sean let him in.

Plopping himself on the floor by Sean's bed, he asked, "What's a wimp?" At fourteen years old, Sean knew everything, or so it seemed to Danny.

"It's someone who's weak and cowardly," said Sean. "Why do you want to know?"

"That's what Em thinks I am. I heard her tell Libby. Do you think I'm a wimp?"

"Nah, I think you're just a little shy, is all." He hesitated. "Listen, can you keep a secret?" Danny nodded solemnly. Sean reached under his bed and pulled out a cloth bundle. He looked straight at Danny. "I got this yesterday, but no one can know I have it. Mom would kill me if she found out about it."

Danny watched Sean unwrap the parcel. Inside was a gleaming pistol, the likes of which he had only seen in video games. He leaned forward. "Is it real?" he whispered.

"Yeah, it is. It's a ghost gun, made here in this city."

"I don't believe it's real. I bet it doesn't shoot real bullets."

"Sure it does. I tested it yesterday."

"I want to test it." Before Sean could blink, Danny grabbed the gun and dashed out of the room, down the stairs, and out of the house.

2

Em woke with a start. She sat up in bed and covered her eyes with her hands. That damn dream again. Would she ever be free of it? She hated reliving that memory from Gloomsbury, the place where she grew up. Her ten-year-old self playing hopscotch in the driveway with her best friend, Libby Lewis. Hearing a shout and looking up. Her 14-year-old brother Sean racing after five-year-old Danny. Sean yelling something at Danny and tackling him. A loud explosion, and Libby motionless on the ground, a red spot blooming on her chest.

She curled her arms around her knees, her heart still beating out of control. A dream was a collection of random thoughts and could be changed. But this was real. It happened, and there was no way to rewrite history. Though Lord knew, she had tried. Fourteen years later, she still felt at the mercy of this nightmare.

"It's not your fault Em," her brother, Sean, had told her again and again. "Libby was in the wrong place at the wrong time."

Yet how could her driveway be the wrong place? It made no sense. In an instant, Em's world had shattered, leaving her with a memory that often woke her at night. Drive-by shootings happened where she grew up, yet she had always felt safe in her own yard and driveway. Sometimes, tensions between street gangs ran high, and her parents did not allow her outside. But this had not been one of those times.

She rubbed her eyes, as she often did on awakening from this nightmare, trying to piece together the forgotten parts of her childhood. Her memory of what happened was fuzzy. She recalled Sean yelling at Danny. Her parents were out, so Sean must've called the police, because soon a single cop car pulled up. Two officers emerged, one black and one white. Em recognized the black cop and was relieved to see him. He had been hired about a year earlier and often patrolled in their predominantly black neighborhood to keep the peace. He was friendly enough to all the black families on the street.

The white policeman, though, was a stranger to her, and his gruff manner made her uneasy. He had close-cropped hair and a wad of chewing gum in his mouth.

Em felt the terror of her ten-year-old self as the two men examined Libby's body. Soon, other officials arrived, and Em watched in horror as they wheeled her friend's lifeless body into the back of the ambulance.

She recalled a heated discussion between Sean and the two policemen. The white officer grilled her brother. "I just need a statement from you, okay? You say a car sped by and whoever was in it must've fired the gun, correct?"

Sean nodded without looking at the man. "Yeah, I saw a man running down the street, dodging parked cars."

That was news to Em. She hadn't noticed a speeding car, and if anyone besides Sean or Danny was running outside, she hadn't seen it.

"Are you sure about this?" the black officer asked. Sean nodded again.

"We got our statement. Leave the boy alone," said the white police officer. His partner shrugged and turned to question Em. But at that moment, her parents showed up and ushered her inside.

Em felt her memory was a giant jigsaw puzzle, and each time this dream occurred more pieces were added. This morning, she recalled how two days after the shooting the black officer had returned to talk to her. She was nervous at first, but he said he wanted to make sure they knew what had happened, for Libby's sake. He faced her in the driveway, as her mother hovered in the background. "Can you tell me what you and your friend were doing?"

"We were playing hopscotch. Right here." She pointed to the chalk squares on the ground.

"Which way was she facing when…"

Em squeezed her eyes closed and tried to remember. "It was her turn. She was here, facing this way."

"Are you positive?" he asked.

"Yeah."

"Did you see a car go by at the time or a man running down the street?"

She shook her head and started to cry. "It was quiet on the street. I didn't see or hear anyone go by."

Em's mom yelled, "Listen, this girl's been through enough trauma. Leave her alone!" She shooed the officer away, and within a week, the family moved from the neighborhood. They spent a few weeks with Em's mom's sister in a cramped one-bedroom apartment before relocating to a small house in a new town. From then on, no one ever discussed what had happened with Em.

"Forget the past," her mom said if the topic ever came up. "We should've moved outta that city long ago."

But Em couldn't forget—at least not completely. The next two years became a blur in the mind of her future self. She vaguely remembered Sean and Danny were inseparable, while she felt like an outsider. The trauma of that day left its mark on them all, especially Danny, changing him from a fun-loving, vibrant kid to a boy who only spoke to his older brother.

The three children shared a mother, but Sean had a different father and fought with his stepfather constantly. After two years, he moved back to the city they grew up in to live with his dad. Danny, at seven years old, refused to talk to any of them, and Sean's father agreed to allow him to join Sean as well. Em was glad to be rid of them both. Secretly, she wondered if Sean's father was also Danny's father, though she was certain her mother would deny it. The idea was ludicrous, given that Sean was four years older than Em, and Danny was five years younger. But the thing was... though they were all black, Em was light-skinned like her mother and father, while both Sean and Danny were blacker than coal, similar to Sean's father. She hadn't spoken to either Sean or Danny since, and now, at twenty-four years old, she wasn't even sure if either of them was still alive.

Em knew what triggered the dream this time. Gun violence was in the news once again. Another mass shooting yesterday—the third in the space of three weeks. Sadly, she shook her head. It had been fourteen years since the death of her friend Libby from a stray bullet, and deadly weapons were still readily available. From mass shootings to gang violence to accidental shootings, it seemed like never a day went by without some grim report. Would it ever stop? To Em, this was a black-and-white issue. As long as the means to commit these violent, horrific acts existed, innocent people would die by gunfire.

She glanced at her clock: 4:30 a.m. She was wide awake now and figured she may as well get up and go to work. As a journalist for the *Post*, a mainstream newspaper, she kept odd hours, and her boss didn't mind as long as she met her deadlines. Often she was the first one into the office in the morning and got her best writing done before the office became a bustling place. She wanted to get off a piece about this latest shooting as soon as possible. Though Em rarely wrote of gun violence, the events of the past few weeks had her re-thinking that. Just yesterday, she had told her boss, Jonathan, that she was considering tackling this issue. Maybe it was time to face those demons. It was the least she could do to honor her childhood friend.

She arrived at the office, surprised to see Jonathan already there. Usually, she had the place to herself for at least an hour.

"What's up?" she asked. "It's not like you to be here so early."

Jonathan stared at her. Something was wrong—she could see it in his eyes.

"Don't start writing yet," he said as she turned on her computer, itching to log in.

"Why not? I want to get out a story about yesterday's shooting. We need to be on top of this one."

"Not so fast," he cautioned her. "I thought you might want to write about this, and I'm getting mixed messages from upper management. You know the paper is under new ownership, right?"

"Of course, but we were told the sale was ceremonial and nothing would change."

"We were told that, but it may not be the case. Our new owners have a different agenda. They don't want us highlighting certain things. Gun violence is on top of their list."

"That's crazy," Em said. "This paper was built around reporting on issues like this. I've written about social justice for my entire career, and this is the most important issue of our time."

"Yeah, well... that's why I'm in early. I need to tell you to tone it down. Libby is being let go."

Em was stunned. "You can't be serious," she said. "They can't fire her—she doesn't even exist."

Jonathan cleared his throat. "Right, well, you know that and I know that, but the new management here doesn't. They don't know who specifically writes as Libby Lewis and they don't care. That persona can no longer write for this paper."

Em stared at her blank computer screen. For two years, she had been a lead journalist for the *Post* and a champion for human rights. She had written about many issues, ranging from corporate greed to online gambling to voting rights. Management had given her free rein to write about a variety of topics, and she wrote most of her articles using her pen name, Libby Lewis. Em did that to hide her own identity from the public. That arrangement had worked perfectly until now.

"So... if they fire Libby, what happens to me?" she asked. The articles she wrote as Emiline Jackson were fillers. Nothing earth-shattering. She usually did the minimum needed to avoid raising any eyebrows among the company executives while focusing the bulk of her work on writing as Libby. She couldn't imagine writing as Emiline full time.

Jonathan shrugged. "I don't know how this will play out. Maybe they'll change their minds, but for now, Libby needs to stand back. I mean it, Em. Don't press your luck with this. I can't keep your identity a secret if you make a stink about it, and you don't want it to get out that you're Libby Lewis."

With a sigh, she realized he was right. She had no way to fight this. Because of the sensitive nature of what Libby wrote about, Em felt it was critical for her true identity to remain separate from her pen name. Still, it irked her. Fourteen years ago, she had lost her best friend. She had promised herself she would be Libby's voice and stand up for those who couldn't speak for themselves. She looked at Jonathan with tears in her eyes.

"Gun violence is something I've wanted to write about for years. It's the reason I do what I do. But I've been afraid. Since I started working here, I've been dancing around it, thinking it was too big, that I needed more experience, more practice, a bigger following. But lately, I've been having this dream. I keep seeing my friend Libby, and I need to be her voice about this. It's time for me to tackle this. I came into work this morning thinking this was it, my next big break, only to be shut down before I could even get started."

"I'm sorry, Em. Truly I am. Things might change in the next few days, but for now, you need to stay away from this issue."

Em fumed all day, while she worked on an article profiling one of Washington's newest restaurants. She couldn't imagine feeling more bored. Since she had come in before sunrise that morning, she left work early, a luxury she rarely took advantage of when pursuing an important story. Dejected, she trudged home. Her mood perked up at the thought of her weekend plans. Typically, Em spent most weekends alone in her apartment. This weekend, however, her college roommate and closest friend, Cara, was hosting a brunch so Em could meet her partner, Ron, who she had recently moved in with. Aside from Jonathan, Cara and Ron were the only friends who knew of her dual identities. Together, they managed a non-profit corporation focusing on gambling addiction, and during the past year, Em (in her persona as Libby) had worked closely with them to uncover corruption in the online gambling industry. However, all the work had been remote, and Em had yet to meet Ron in person.

Em had promised to bring something for brunch that Cara had raved about in the past. Hopefully, Ron would feel the same. Em loved introducing her white friends to foods they would normally never eat. Shrimp and grits, along with banana pudding, she thought. Cooking soothed her, especially when she could listen to music. In the privacy of her home, she put on her favorite music by Beyoncé and set to work in the kitchen. The perfect blend of rhythm and blues, soul, pop, and hip hop, along with the tantalizing odor of peppers, garlic and onions, calmed her frayed nerves. As she cooked, she thought of her friends. Both Cara and Ron had lost their jobs at the CDC (Centers for Disease Control) because they had attempted to research some things that were considered off limits. Em felt they would understand her dilemma and was grateful she could turn to them. She looked forward to being with them, though she grudgingly realized she needed their advice more than she cared to admit.

3

By the time Em arrived at Ron and Cara's house the next day, she had once again worked herself into a rage.

"I can't believe they fired Libby! How could they do that?" she seethed, pacing back and forth on the porch.

"It was great to work with you as Libby and I'm sorry to see her go," said Ron. "But look at it this way. At least you still have a job and a paycheck coming in."

"But what good is it if I can't write what I want?" she asked. "There's nothing more boring than writing about restaurants and fashion! If I can't write about stuff that matters to me, then I quit!"

"I'm going to give you the exact advice you gave me last year," Cara chimed in. "Do your job like you're supposed to and lay the groundwork for what's next."

"But what is next?" wailed Em. "I spent all this time developing a reputation as Libby Lewis, and that's being snatched away. She's gone—'poof'—and since no one knows I was her, I can't use that identity if I apply for future jobs. No one would want to hire Emiline Jackson. All she writes is boring run-of-the-mill stuff with no imagination. She has no portfolio to speak of. Where would I even begin to look for a new job?"

"Well, for one thing, you could open a restaurant," said Ron. "This food you brought is amazing! I don't think I've ever tasted anything quite like it."

Cara nodded in agreement. "I told you she was a woman of many talents!"

Em glared at them both. "Cooking is something I do for me, to calm myself down. I'm glad you like it, but it's not like I could ever make a living out of that. Journalism is my life."

"Okay, so if you want to keep writing, what about launching your own non-profit news site?" asked Ron. "There are a lot of resources out there to help with that." He pulled out his phone and began scrolling through it.

"You're kidding, right? Me, launch my own news site? I don't know the first thing about business or how to do that."

"Sure you do!" chimed in Cara. "You've been involved with our company since the beginning! You helped us get it off the ground, and we can help you now."

Em sat and hugged her knees. She had never been one to accept handouts. She shook her head. "You two have enough on your plate. I can't ask you to help me like that."

"You're not asking. We're offering," said Cara. "You are way more capable than you give yourself credit for. If this is something you truly want, you can do this. You once told me: 'the bigger the risk, the bigger the payout.' This is a big risk for you, and maybe it's time."

Ron showed her his phone. "Here, look at this. It's a link to an organization dedicated to helping reporters and journalists start up their own non-profit news agency. You could start up a news magazine. It has a step-by-step guide." Em glanced at it, then pushed the phone away. She stood up and paced again. "Send me the link and I'll look at it," she said glumly.

"I think Ron may be on to something. Keep your identity as Libby. You've put a lot of effort into building a following using her name. You should run with that. How about you talk with Henry Ives? After all, he's a master at changing identities, and he might be able to give you some pointers."

Em pondered that. Through the work she had done with Cara and Ron, she knew Henry remotely in the same way she knew Ron. He, too, had worked at the CDC and had teamed up with Cara and Ron to investigate some key ring-leaders in online gambling corporations. He was a brilliant computer programmer who had maintained several different identities in his life. They all knew him as Henry, though his given name was James, and now he often went under the name Samuel. Cara was right—Henry knew about changing identities. Would that be helpful to her? Though Libby was her pen name, she didn't consider it a real identity. Yet maybe it was. The thought of Libby being fired angered her to no end. It felt like they fired *her*. Did she actually consider herself to *be* Libby? Or did the possibility of losing her connection to Libby bother her? Or... was she hiding behind the guise of Libby, so she didn't have to put her real self at risk?

"This is so confusing!" she lamented. "I want to speak for Libby, but I'm not sure I want to fully take on her identity."

"Talk to Henry," urged Cara. "One conversation can't hurt. Maybe he can help you sort some of this out. And think about striking out on your own. You can make a name for yourself independent of the newspaper."

Em looked at her friend, who seemed so sure of herself. It wasn't long ago that Cara was feeling lost and seeking Em's advice. Em was used to being the wise one in their relationship. Somehow, this reversal of roles felt awkward, yet she knew Cara was right. It was time to make some changes in her life. For too long, she had held back from writing what was truly in her heart, and if her employer would not allow it, then she needed to take matters into her own hands.

***

Alone in her apartment, Em browsed the internet, intrigued by the link Ron had sent. Could she create an online magazine dedicated to telling the stories of underprivileged people? After all, that was what she had been doing at the *Post* for the past two years, though the administrative part of it hadn't been her responsibility. How hard could it be?

Step one was "Define Your Mission," and she spent the better part of the morning on that, becoming more excited with every word she wrote. The possibility of continuing to write as Libby Lewis fired her up. Libby was an integral part of her, and she needed to figure out how that might work in the future. Having a pen name was tricky enough, but if the publication she intended to put forth was hers and hers alone, could she do it under Libby's name? Or should the official public face be Emiline, with Libby as a ghostwriter? She still needed to sort all this out.

Maybe I should talk to Henry, she thought. Much as she didn't like taking advice from others, she realized she was stuck. But one thing worried her. She reached for her phone and called Cara.

"I've been thinking of calling Henry, but I'm just not sure," she told her friend. "He makes me nervous."

"Henry's okay. Sometimes he comes across as a little odd, but he's a sweet guy. It took me a while to get to know him, but now that I do, I can say there's more to him than meets the eye. His experience with changing identities could be a big help for you. What makes you nervous?"

"I just feel uncomfortable around him," Em said. "For one thing, I did a background check on him last year, remember?

I learned he has a gun permit. I hate guns!" She looked at the phone, momentarily surprised by her own outburst.

Cara paused, thinking back to her time at the CDC where she and Henry had worked together in the same office. She was sure Henry never had a gun with him when she was with him. True, he had a complicated history, but Cara felt confident he would never hurt anyone.

"Em, lots of people have gun permits. That doesn't mean he carries a gun with him all the time. If you're concerned about it, why not ask him about it?"

Em considered that. The dream the other night had really affected her, she realized. It wasn't the first time she'd dreamt about Libby—far from it. However, this time felt more real. Somehow, it gripped her and wouldn't let go. Maybe she should ask Henry to leave his gun at home, but she didn't want to have to explain why. "I'll think about it," she mumbled to Cara.

"Good," replied Cara. "Listen, don't worry so much. You have an incredible talent for journalistic writing and will find an outlet for it. I know you, and I know what you're capable of. Let us help you. Let Henry help you if he wants to. Just because the *Post* wants to stop Libby doesn't mean she's gone. Many times, you told me you wanted to be her voice, and now is as good a time as any to bring that forward. I love Ron's idea of you starting your own magazine. If anyone can do it, you can."

Em hesitated. Unlike Ron, Henry knew her only as Libby. If she wanted to get his advice on managing her identity, she'd have to tell him about her dual identities as well. That worried her. She had put so much effort into keeping Libby private, and the thought of letting anyone else in on her secret terrified her.

Em sighed. "Maybe you're right, but Henry only knows me as Libby. It feels weird to talk to him as Em. For now, I'm going to keep my day job at the *Post,* so money keeps coming in. I'll let you know if that changes."

What the hell? she thought after getting off the phone with Cara. *If Libby no longer exists, it probably doesn't matter!* But what if she wanted to keep Libby alive? She covered her face with her hands. *Why was this so complicated?*

She reached for her secure phone that she only used for "Libby business." She knew Henry's phone was secure as well. It was time to start trusting people if she was going to get any kind of support. Picking up the phone, she called Henry. He answered immediately.

"Hey, Libby! I haven't heard from you in a while. What's up?"

Em was momentarily tongue-tied. She hadn't expected him to answer right away, and she thought she'd have more time to collect her thoughts. After all, in the past, they had only interacted about business-related things, and this was a very personal thing she was calling about. "Er... I saw Cara yesterday, and she suggested I talk to you to get some advice."

"Cara told you to get advice from me? That's a first. About what?"

"It has to do with changing identities. I'm not real comfortable talking about this on the phone. Can we meet somewhere and I can give you a little more information?"

"Sure. My schedule is probably a bit more flexible than yours. You pick the time and place."

She took a deep breath. Truth be told, she hated going out in public, but it was better to meet him in a public place than privately, especially if he might be carrying a gun. She knew she was being paranoid, but she couldn't shake the feeling of dread. Nevertheless, she had called him and initiated the invitation. There was no backing down now. She gave him the name of a crowded café across town. "I'm taking a day off work tomorrow. Can you meet in the morning for coffee?"

Henry agreed, and Em bit her lip, hoping this wasn't a big mistake. "One more thing... you should know that in public, I'm not Libby. Libby is a pen name. You should call me 'Em.'"

"M? As in the letter? Does it stand for anything?"

"No, that's my name! E - M, short for Emiline."

"Okay, Emiline. I will see you tomorrow. You have my curiosity up now!"

4

Em glanced around the crowded café, taking in the modern decor and quiet music in the background. Tastefully done, she thought. Plenty of space for people to gather, with private booths as well. If she kept her job at the *Post*, this would be a place worth reviewing.

She had chosen this coffee shop because it was in one of the more diverse areas of the city, and looking around at the smattering of people of all ethnicities, she breathed a sigh of relief. A young Asian woman sat across from a guy with bright orange hair in a long ponytail. Definitely a couple, Em thought, judging by their body language. No one around them seemed to care. She knew from experience that even in this day and age, the sight of a black woman with a white man might draw attention, which was the last thing she wanted. She ordered a cup of coffee at the counter and looked around again, wondering how she would recognize Henry. Though she had talked with him on the phone countless times, she had never met him in person. A text came in on her phone: **"I'm**

in a booth in the back. Is that you who just came in?"
A short, skinny white man stood and signaled to her. As she
slid onto the bench opposite him, she took a moment to assess
him. Cara had told her he used to look like a total slob, but Em
thought he looked quite put-together now. She noticed he was
fidgeting with some beads in his hands. He quickly put them
away in his pocket. He seemed nervous, or maybe that was just
his nature. Briefly, she wondered if he had his gun on him, but
she pushed that thought aside.

"Hi," he said. "I'm glad to meet you in person after all this
time. Though it feels like I know you well already."

Em squirmed. *He knew Libby well. But did he know Em at
all?* "I don't like to be around people in public," she declared.
"In my line of work, I need to keep a low profile." *Libby needs
to keep a low profile was what she really should have said.*

Henry nodded. "I can understand that. So, what brings you
here now? You said you wanted some advice about changing
identities."

His directness surprised her. Nervously, her eyes darted
around the diner to reassure herself no one could overhear
their conversation. "I have one identity. I'm Em. That's the
name on my driver's license, and the lease on my apartment.
That's my name at work, as well, unless I write something
controversial. Then I use my pen name, Libby. No one at work
knows that except my direct boss. He's covered for me for

two years. It worked beautifully, until last week, when new management took over and changed the focus of the paper. They 'fired' Libby, telling my boss that whoever was writing as Libby should stop writing those controversial articles. I can still work there as Emiline, writing boring articles about restaurants and fashion, but Libby Lewis can no longer write about social justice or anything meaningful."

Henry gave a low whistle. "Wait... so Libby was just a made-up persona of yours? Why that name?"

Again, Em looked around. This line of questioning made her uncomfortable and was not a topic she usually discussed. She looked down, half hoping he would go away, but when she raised her eyes, he was still there, looking at her expectantly. *You initiated this,* she reminded herself. If only she could get up and pace the floor. She thought best when pacing. She sighed.

"Okay, if you must know, Libby was a childhood friend of mine. Best friend, actually. We were 10 years old, playing in the driveway of my house when a stray bullet killed her. Gang violence. At least that's what my older brother told me." She quickly swiped a tear from her eye with her sleeve and looked around again, staring at everything but him.

"Interesting...," said Henry. "So you took on her name to be her voice?"

She looked at him now, surprised by his response. No *'Sorry,'* or *'That's too bad.'* Cara was right. Henry was a bit odd, and sympathy wasn't his strong point. Yet, in a way, Em was glad. She didn't want anyone's pity.

"I guess I did. I tell myself that's when I decided to become a journalist. Honestly, I remember little of that time. My family moved immediately after. My mom wanted to get out of that city, and she pushed me to go to school and then on to a mostly white college. That's where I met Cara. We were roommates there, and she helped me navigate a more diverse environment. I buried myself in school, and then after I graduated, I wanted a different experience, so I went to Howard University to get a master's degree in journalism, which reinforced my desire to write about social issues. When I got the job at the *Post*, it seemed natural to use Libby's name. My boss agreed, and after a while, the name became protective, since Libby got hate mail whenever she wrote controversial stuff."

"Do you ever feel you are her? Or is it just that she speaks through you?"

Em cocked her head in thought. No one had ever asked her that before. "I don't know," she said slowly. "Mostly, she speaks to me through my writing, though occasionally, I have this dream...." She paused, unsure how much she wanted to reveal. Henry waited without saying a word.

"It's not really a dream. It's a memory of that day. And it's always the same. Libby and I are playing hopscotch on the driveway, then my older brother, Sean, runs out of the house chasing my younger brother. The next thing I know, Libby is lying there, shot in the chest. It's like a rerun of a bad movie over and over. Always exactly the same footage with nothing before and nothing after. I don't have any other memories of my childhood after that for at least another two years, when I entered middle school. It's all a blank."

"You ever talk to your brother about it?" he asked.

"Sean?" she shook her head sadly. "No, never. He told me it wasn't my fault—she was just in the wrong place at the wrong time. Sean was four years older than me and, from what I remember, he was always angry. He and my parents fought a lot. He's actually my half-brother. My dad was his stepdad, and they didn't get along. After a while, he moved back to Gloomsbury to live with his natural dad, and I haven't talked to him since. So, no... we never talked about it." She squeezed her eyes closed, wishing she was anyplace else but here.

"What about your younger brother?"

"Danny?" she asked. "I haven't seen him in years either. He's nineteen now. He was pretty traumatized by the whole thing and stopped talking to everyone except Sean. He left home shortly after Sean did and followed Sean to Gloomsbury. As far as I know, they're still there. But they could both be dead now. It wouldn't surprise me, with all the gun violence that goes on there."

"Sorry," said Henry. "I didn't mean to open up some old wounds."

"Yeah, well, you weren't the one who opened them. I did, by calling you. Now you know why I took on the persona of Libby." She paused and looked squarely at him. He had been calling the shots, asking all the questions. "It's my turn to ask you something," she continued. He nodded, motioning for her to go ahead. "Why do you have a gun permit?"

He sat back, surprised. "First, I don't carry a gun all the time. I don't have it with me right now." He held out his open hands toward her, as if to emphasize the point. "I got it for self-defense after I left Senator Bly's office, and I have a valid license to carry it. But also, I grew up around guns. My grandfather hunted and took me with him whenever we visited his farm. He taught me how to shoot and be safe around firearms."

She shook her head. "There's just no place in the world for guns. I can't see it. As long as they exist, no one is safe."

"Is that what your friend Libby is telling you?" he asked. "Because I'm not sure that's completely true."

"Of course it's true!" she declared, gripping her coffee cup tightly. "She'd still be alive right now if there were no guns on the streets."

"Okay, maybe. I don't want to get into a whole debate with you about gun rights. Not now, anyway. I am happy to talk to you about this whole identity thing, though. I have a bit of experience with that, you know."

Em nodded. She knew his given name was James, and he had a twin brother, Henry, who died several years ago. James changed his name to Henry to hide from his former employer, Senator Bly, after witnessing a scandal involving the senator. And then just last year, he took on another identity for his work, in the same way she used Libby as a pen name. She looked at him now. "Do you ever feel you are your brother?"

Henry sat back. "Nah, not anymore. I used to at first. When I began using his name, I felt like I was in his skin, or maybe he was in my skin. But now, we've kind of melded into one. We were twins, so there wasn't much of a boundary between us. Working with Cara helped as well, and Senator Bly's arrest lifted a huge load off my shoulders. It was like my brother finally let go, and I was now free to live my own life. I could go back to being James now, but I rather enjoy being Henry."

"And Samuel?" she asked.

His eyes widened. Now it was his turn to be surprised. "How do you know about him?"

"C'mon. You know Cara and I talk. There are no secrets between us," she said.

"If you must know, I reserve Samuel for work only. The work I'm doing for Cara requires me to log in and get cozy with some online corporations so I can get information. As Samuel,

I've been able to infiltrate some online gambling sites and I get more information all the time. That's a reputation I need to protect. It's very much like your pen name."

Em nodded. "Could you help me be Libby?" she asked impulsively. "I mean, actually be her. Like with a driver's license, credit cards, all that stuff? How hard is it?"

"It's really quite simple. But you need to think hard about why you're doing it and when you would use it. Otherwise, life could get very complicated."

"Libby had a huge following, and Em has none of that. Ron showed me a website which talked about how to build a business by developing a non-profit news agency. When I looked at it, I thought I wasn't qualified, but Libby would be. If I could start a business in her name, I could continue to write as her," she said.

"I could help you change your identity, but I'm not sure you need to do that. Why not simply stay as Em, but continue to write as Libby like you've been doing?"

"Because it's so hard, having a double life. When I'm working on a story, I feel like I have to hide my true self, because if anyone finds out who I am, my life might be in danger. Libby got so much hate mail at the *Post* whenever I attacked an industry or someone felt threatened. Her identity needed to be kept secret."

"Em, that won't change if you become Libby. The hate mail will still come, and you'll have even more exposure. Using Libby as a pen name is a brilliant idea, and I don't think you should do it any differently. I know living a double life is tough, but you shouldn't give up your identity as Em unless you need to hide from someone specific, as I did from Senator Bly. As for your own non-profit news agency, I love that idea."

"You really think so?" she asked. "Because I have a hard time seeing it."

"I do think so. That could be a tremendous success and it would belong to Em. Let Libby be your public voice, but don't hide who Em is. Maybe you can't see it now, but if you don't try, you'll never know. I'm happy to help you navigate the dual identities with one condition."

"What condition?" she asked, narrowing her eyes.

"If you want to write about guns and gun control, you need to learn about them. I mean, really learn. How do they work? Why are people so drawn to them? Let me teach you how to use a gun, and I'll work with you to create a new public identity as Libby Lewis—one that is separate from Em but doesn't replace her."

Em felt her anger flare. *Who the hell did he think he was, asking her to learn to use a gun?* There was no way she could go for that.

"I think we're done here," she said flatly, getting up to leave. "Forget it. It'll never happen."

Henry clutched the metal balls in his hands and looked at her. "Your choice," he said. "You know how to reach me if you change your mind."

5

Back in her apartment, Em paced the floor. The conversation with Henry had rattled her, and pacing helped calm her nerves. "You need to get inside a shooter's head in order to write about them. Learning to handle a gun is the best way to do that," he had said.

Em pondered that now. Maybe it would give her a new angle to work with, but the thought of actually picking up a firearm terrified her. She stood still, closed her eyes, and all she could see was Libby lying on the driveway. She wasn't sure she could get past that image and actually hold a gun in her hand. With her eyes closed, her mind drifted back, and once again, she wondered what really happened that day. Henry had asked her if she had ever talked to Sean about it, and her response had been immediate. Now, though, she recalled the few times she had tried to talk to him and he had refused. He simply told her it wasn't her fault and to quit thinking about it. Aside from her brother Danny, who was only five years old at the time, Sean was the only one who could fill in the blanks in her memory.

Perhaps if she talked to Sean now, as an adult, he could provide her with more information.

Henry had mentioned opening old wounds. She had worked hard to keep those wounds covered, but maybe it was time to peel off the Band-Aids and see what was underneath. It wouldn't be hard to track her brother down, she thought.

She looked at the link Ron had sent her. The pull to start her own online publication felt so powerful. What was she hoping to accomplish? She sat at her desk, opened her laptop, and jotted down some notes.

My Mission:

To advocate for social justice.

To be a voice for those who can't speak for themselves.

To examine the systems in our country that keep people oppressed.

To come up with solutions and ways for meaningful change to happen.

As she wrote, she realized she had already been doing this for the past two years as Libby. She had written on a variety of topics, and her following was huge. It wouldn't be hard to bring people over to a new platform. The first thing she wanted to focus on now was gun violence. Was Henry right? Could she write about guns effectively without knowing how they work? Clearly, she had a bias against them. Every day, guns killed innocent people. A gun killed Libby. Take away guns, and Libby would still be alive. There was no other way to look at it. Yet, Henry had a good point. To truly reach people, maybe she needed a broader understanding.

The thought of handling a gun made her stomach clench to the point she felt physically ill. This was why she hadn't yet written about guns. Both her identities argued in her head.

Libby: *It's time for you to write about gun violence!*

Em: *I know! But I don't know where to start.*

Libby: *You'll be much more persuasive if you learn more about guns. Let Henry teach you!*

Em: *I don't want to be near a gun! That's what killed you!*

Libby: *Yes, a gun killed me. But you need to understand what really happened. Research this! Learn about guns. Open your eyes and look at the big picture. Henry can help with that. And talk to your brother!*

Shaking, she opened her eyes. Understand what really happened? What the hell did that mean? Henry was right. Old wounds were open now, and there was no turning back. With a sigh, she picked up her phone and called Henry. He answered immediately.

Em took a deep breath. "I've been thinking about what you said... about how I need to learn more about guns in order to write more effectively about gun control. I'm willing to try it. Can you teach me?" She imagined his smile on the other end of the call to distract her from her nausea.

"Sure! I'd be happy to. You pick the time."

"As soon as you're available, so I don't back out," she found herself saying. She was already having second thoughts about it. They settled on a time the next day, and Em ended the call, feeling completely drained.

***

She approached Henry's apartment with trepidation. He had suggested she come to his place for her first lesson. Although she trusted him, she felt nervous being alone with a man in his house, especially knowing he had a gun in that house. A gun that he was going to teach her to use. Would she really be safe? Feeling a tiny bit foolish, she called Cara.

"You'll be fine," Cara reassured her. "Henry won't hurt you. It's good he's willing to teach you. He's a straight-forward guy. He wants to help. Let him."

Henry lived in the downtown area of the city. His apartment was small, and the computer monitor filling one wall of the living room astonished her. She knew his work involved research into Virtual Reality, so it shouldn't have surprised her, but she'd never seen a monitor that large before.

"Are you Libby or Em for this?" he asked when she arrived.

"Does it matter?"

"Maybe not, but I want to know what to call you."

She pondered that for a moment. Was she really two different people? Henry was forcing her to think about her relationship with Libby in an entirely new way. "I'm Em," she announced. "I may eventually write about this under Libby's name, but Em's the one who needs to learn about it."

"Okay, there's an entire culture around guns you need to learn about," he said. "I thought we'd start with video games. You may know this already, but I want you to understand what society exposes kids to at a very early age. Many of these games get kids to think of guns as toys. Let's play a few and you can see for yourself."

Henry motioned for her to sit and gave her a console. "Have you played any video games in the past?"

She shook her head.

He looked at her in disbelief. "You had two brothers and never played video games? How is that possible?"

Em looked away. "I guess Sean and Danny played them before," she mumbled. "But after Libby, everything changed. After we moved, my parents banned video games from the house. I never had an interest."

"Well then, this will be a new learning experience for you," he said. "I'm sure you know a huge percentage of children play video games every day. It's a big influence on their lives. We'll start with some of the more benign games for younger kids before moving up to the violent ones. First, you need an image for your avatar. This will be your character in the game. It represents you." He clicked his mouse, and the screen was filled with images of kids of all sizes. "For some games, your avatar can be an animal, or even an inanimate object, but this game uses kids. Go ahead and pick one you identify with."

Em nodded. She hadn't expected to learn about guns through games, but if Henry thought this made sense, then she'd go along with it. She scrolled through the images and settled on a young, light-skinned black girl with short, kinky dark hair. The girl reminded her of Libby at age 10.

"Okay, now you need to give it a screen name."

"What's your screen name?" she asked.

"Parsley," he said.

"Parsley?" she said with a laugh. "Where did that come from?"

"I don't know... I made it up when I was a kid years ago and it stuck. My mom forced me to eat parsley because it was good for me. I never had a reason to change it. It does kind of become like another identity. Pick something you can identify with."

Em closed her eyes and thought for a moment. "Delfino," she announced. It seemed to slide off her tongue.

Henry raised his eyebrows in question.

"It was one of the last things Libby and I learned about together in school, when we were 10 years old. It comes from Latin and refers to dolphins, which were considered a symbol of goodness and friendliness in medieval times."

"Okay—Delfino it is. Let's see... for this game, Delfino needs to be on a quest of some sort. Your avatar collects things. He showed her a list of things available for collection. Parsley's collecting books. What do you want to collect?"

"Flowers!" said Em with a smile.

Em was shocked at how quickly the game drew her in and how much fun it was. As the game experience took over, she forgot about the outside world. She enjoyed moving Delfino around, exploring the territory, gathering flowers, and amassing tools.

"What just happened?" She blinked as her avatar suddenly disappeared.

"Delfino stepped into a minefield. You lost one life."

"You're kidding, right? I thought you said this is a game for little kids!"

"Welcome to the world of video gaming," he said softly. "Nothing is sacred here... especially life."

Em had nothing to say about that. She concentrated on avoiding the minefields and collecting more flowers and tools. Most of the tools were useful for things like building and gardening, but she could see how some might be weapons as well. She laughed as Henry's avatar, Parsley, approached her and challenged her to a duel. She accepted and was shocked to see it was a fight to the death. Another life lost. "How many lives do you get in this game?" she asked.

"It depends. In the mode we're playing in, it's unlimited. Many games work that way. If they limited the number of lives, kids might stop playing, and the game creators don't want that."

"So, they feed kids this idea that it's no big deal to lose your life since you simply get back up and keep playing?"

"More or less, yeah," Henry replied. "They build in a few consequences for losing lives, like maybe you end up owing something to another player, or you lose points. But in terms of real consequences, you are exactly right. In most video games, there are no major consequences for losing your life—or for taking the life of another player."

Em was astounded at how skilled she got after playing for a few hours. By the end of the session, she had graduated in rank to a "two-star player." She also couldn't believe how much fun it was. She felt like she was inside a play in which she was the playwright, director and actor all at once. What power she had! Once she got used to the idea of multiple lives, she found she could let go and simply enjoy herself. Her avatar and Henry's teamed up and were collecting items for a planned expedition.

She was having a great time... until Parsley showed up with a gun.

"I think we'll stop here," said Henry, rising and turning the game console off. "I don't want to throw too much at you at once."

"That's it?" she said, disappointment tinging her voice.

"For today, yeah," he said. "Go home and think about everything you saw today. Let it simmer in your head for a few days. I want you to be really comfortable with all this before we graduate to real guns. Keep in mind—this is what many, many teenagers are doing these days, every day after school. Kids today rarely play outside with sticks and stones. They much prefer to live in these virtual games."

And why not? she thought. The instant gratification was immensely fulfilling. The game designers wanted you to succeed.

The concept of multiple lives floored her. If you died in a video game, you simply used up one of your multiple lives without consequence. Yet there was an enormous disconnect between the games and the real world. Em could see how playing these games over and over could warp your view of reality, especially if you were a young kid. How much difference was there, really, between shooting a person online and shooting them for real? A world of difference in her mind, but a young child raised on video games might not view it that way.

"The games are getting more and more real each day. This is part of what I have been working on with Cara—trying to curb the use of VR (virtual reality) in the gaming industry. It's not the only cause, but it's one of the roots of gun violence. This is so culturally embedded into our children these days."

"So... you're already working with Cara on gun violence? She never told me."

Henry paused. "Er... that may be because she doesn't know exactly what I've been doing here. I figure it's all connected, see? I have a contract with her to infiltrate many of these sites and monitor the impact of Virtual Reality. Whether it's drawing customers in to gamble, or promoting violence, it's all about distorting reality."

"You're right," Em said. "I never looked at it this way before. I dreaded coming here today, but now I see I have a lot to learn. Gun violence has always been such an all-or-nothing issue for me."

"Well, I hope you'll say the same thing once we graduate to real guns," he replied. Em flinched. "But don't fret about that yet. We'll have a couple more video sessions before we get there."

6

True to his word, Henry invited her back for several more video sessions which grew increasingly violent. At first, the violence repulsed her, but over time she became captivated and obsessed with moving up in the rankings. Even with the violence, she could see how the developers crafted the games to still be games. Winning was all about rankings, and life or death meant little. In fact, often being killed in a game gave you a higher ranking! The more she played, the more Em saw how these games had the potential to warp the minds of an entire generation of children. Through the haze of her blunted childhood memory, she recalled times before Libby, when Sean and Danny played video games together. Danny had only been five years old! How had this affected him?

Finally, Henry announced that their next session would be at the shooting range to experience real guns.

"I'm not sure I'm ready," Em told him.

Now, she paced in her apartment, contemplating what she had learned. Should she continue on this path? What would it be like to hold an actual gun in her hand? She stopped pacing and sat at her desk. Besides pacing, the thing that most helped her sort through her feelings was writing. Though she had kept her day job at the *Post*, she hadn't given up on the idea of creating her own online news magazine. She already had a list of topics she wanted to cover. She looked it over now.

Illegal gun ownership.
The connection of guns to money... Who profits?
Is there a "gun kingpin" comparable to a drug lord?
Why haven't gun laws passed? Is it just political? Or racist?
Is it more about politics, or more about money?

She read over the list and added another:
Why are guns allowed around kids?

Sean had a gun. Where did it come from? The sudden memory of that ripped through her. She hadn't thought of it in years. But now, she recalled with crystal clarity seeing him show off a small pistol to his friends the day before Libby was shot. Where did it go?

As if in a trance, she heard Libby's voice once again:

"I told you to find your brother Sean and talk to him! Why haven't you done that yet?"

"I've been busy learning about guns from Henry! You told me to do that as well!"

"Right, I did, but it's more important for you to learn what really happened that day. Sean is the only one who can tell you. Find him!"

And as quickly as the voice came, it disappeared. What was she supposed to do with *that*?

She reached for her phone and called Henry. They had plans to go to the shooting range the next day, but she didn't feel ready yet. She needed to tell him that and also wanted his advice on how to deal with Libby. After all, he had told her he would help her create Libby as a separate identity. The voice had seemed so real, as if Libby was actually communicating with her. Was that possible?

Once again, he picked up his phone immediately. "What's up, Em?" he asked.

This time, she was more prepared. "Libby spoke to me," she said, matter-of-factly.

"Really?" He sounded intrigued. "What did she say?"

"She told me to find my brother, Sean, and learn what really happened that day. She insisted I need to know, and he is the only one who can tell me. I want to do that this weekend, so can we postpone our trip to the shooting range?"

"Okay," said Henry slowly. "Do you have any idea where Sean is?"

"No, but I have the tools to find him. Remember... I work at the *Post*, and even though I'm no longer an investigative reporter there, I still can get that kind of information. He won't be hard to find."

Henry was silent for a moment. "You know, you don't have to do everything Libby says."

"That's why I called you. You told me you could help me navigate these dual identities. I'm having trouble separating from her. Is she really speaking to me? Or is it my subconscious telling me? And does that even matter?"

Henry sighed. "Em, I know what it's like to become that person who died—to take on their identity and be their voice. To want to be in their head, think their thoughts. But ultimately, we can't do that."

She shook her head, tears streaming down her face. "We can! I can! This is what she wants me to do!"

"Maybe... but more important is 'What do you want to do?' This is about your life, not Libby's. Maybe you have the same desires as Libby and maybe not. *You* are the one alive now, and you need to figure out your life first. What does Em want?"

She stared at the phone. She had never asked herself that before. "I want to live in a world where kids aren't afraid to play in their own front yards. A world without hatred and violence. Is that too much to ask?"

"And you think that taking away all the guns will fix that? Will that take away hatred as well? Because until our culture changes, it doesn't matter what the weapons are. That's what I've been trying to show you."

Em paused. He was right, she realized. There needed to be a cultural shift, but she felt powerless to create it. Yet Libby's voice seemed to be telling her that would change if she reconnected with her past. And Sean was her key to the past. What was the harm in listening to Libby? "I want to understand all this better," she told him. "And if talking to my brother will help me do that, then that's what I need to do." She paused again. "For Em," she added. "Not for Libby."

"Well, there's your answer, then. I'm glad you figured it out. Keep me posted."

7

Em stood on the street corner and re-checked the address on her phone. It was definitely the garage where her brother, Sean, worked. One advantage of working as an investigative reporter for a major newspaper was she had a lot of resources at her disposal. It hadn't taken her long to locate her brother Sean—working at an auto-body shop close to the neighborhood where she grew up.

Danny, on the other hand, was proving harder to find. As far as she could tell, he was still alive. At least nobody had filed a death certificate with his name. No job listings or residences either. She had fully expected some sort of criminal record, but found nothing. Maybe Sean could tell her. She stood a short distance from the door, hoping to get a glimpse of him before going in. Twelve years had passed since she last saw him, and she wondered if she would recognize him.

Two mechanics came out together, chatting. One was short and heavy-set, definitely not her brother. The Sean she remembered was tall, dark, lean and muscular, even at age 16.

The taller man had his hair in dreadlocks and looked to be about Sean's current age. She closed her eyes briefly, trying to conjure up a picture of her brother in her mind. Was it him? The answer came a moment later, when he glanced her way and then stared straight at her, hard. She may not have identified him, but he recognized her. He blinked, shook his head, and looked again.

"Em?" he blurted out. "What the hell you doin' here?"

"I came to see you," she said. Though she had rehearsed this over and over during the past few days, it still sounded stilted.

"Well, this is sure a surprise!" He turned to his co-worker. "Bobby, meet my little sister, Em!"

"I never knew you had a sister! She don' look like you at all! How come you never mentioned her before?" asked Bobby, eying her up and down with appreciation.

"You never asked. Anyway, she's my half-sister, and we haven't seen each other for... how long now?" He looked at Em.

"It's been twelve years, Sean," she spat out.

"Yeah, that's what I thought. We haven't talked in a long time. What brings you here?" He peered at her anxiously. "Is there a problem with Ma?"

As if you really cared. You disappeared with no forwarding address. "Ma's okay. We don't talk much these days. She doesn't know I'm here."

Sean studied her. "You look like her," he said. "You're all grown up. Last I remember, you was just a scrawny and scared little girl."

"Yeah, well, we all grow up eventually." She took a breath in and looked squarely at him. "I need some answers, Sean."

"About what?" he asked.

"About Libby. What happened that day?"

She saw him stiffen before turning to his buddy. "Bobby, I need to talk to my sister here for a bit. Can you handle things here if I take a quick break?"

"Sure," said Bobby, going into the garage.

Sean turned back to Em. "C'mon, let's go for a walk." He started down the street, and she fell into step beside him. They walked in silence past several blocks of dilapidated, abandoned apartments with boarded-up windows. The street was devoid of people, save for a few beggars lounging in stairwells to stay out of the sun. Em wondered if anyone actually lived here. The only evidence of human habitation was trash strewn everywhere. But when she looked closer, she saw a child peeking out from behind drawn curtains on one of the upper floors. She shivered. *What a way to grow up.* She remembered very little of her childhood, but what she did recall wasn't like this. Most of the time, she had felt comfortable playing outside her house. Until....

"Why you want to bring up ancient history, Em?" he asked.

"I want to know what happened to Libby, and you're the only one who can tell me. I keep having this dream, and it's like a bad TV rerun—every night, the same scene. You and Danny come running out of the house, and then—'Boom!'—she's gone. You told the police you saw someone running by, but I didn't see anyone. All these years, I've been wondering if you were covering something up. I need to find out... do you know who shot Libby?"

Sean glanced at her, then looked at the sky. "I don't want to talk about this with you," he said. Hands in his pockets, he turned away from her and started back toward the shop.

"Wait!" she cried. "Can't you tell me anything?"

He paused and turned around to stare at her. For a moment, he closed his eyes. When he opened them, he seemed focused on something far away.

"I fucked up," he whispered.

"What?" she asked, craning her head toward him. She wasn't sure she heard him correctly. *Was it possible he had fired that gun?*

"I said, I fucked up." His expression. might have been pain, anger, sadness, or a mixture of all three. "Let's just say it was someone who shouldn't have had a gun," he finally said.

"What do you mean? Who shot her?"

Sean resumed walking without looking at her. "I was hoping we'd never have this conversation," he said.

"What are you talking about, Sean?" she demanded.

"It was Danny," he whispered.

Em stopped dead in her tracks. "Danny? He fired that gun? How is that even possible? He was five years old! What the hell was he doing with a gun?"

Sean looked at her now, and she saw the pain etched on his face. "It was my fault. I got a brand-new gun the day before and I was so excited. Before Danny came into the room, I loaded it, then hid it away. I pulled it out to show it to him, like I was so important. Danny and I—we had been playing these video games all week, and his little head was filled with pictures of guns. He was going around everywhere, pretendin' to shoot everyone and everything. When Danny saw the gun, he went crazy over it! Wanted to hold it, feel it. I was so stupid—I let him grab it from my hand. Then he took off, running down the stairs and out of the house. He had no idea what he was doing. To him, it was all a game. I saw him take aim at you and Libby, and I tackled him, but it was too late."

Em sank down and sat on the steps of an apartment building. She buried her head in her hands. All these years, she thought Libby was simply a victim of a random shooting, a drive-by-gang member targeting someone else. The thought of her younger brother holding that gun was unfathomable to her. "I can't believe this!" she sobbed. "You knew all along! You knew it was Danny, and you hid it from everyone! Why?"

"What good would it have done to say anything?" he blurt-ed. "The gun was illegal. At fourteen years old, I should never have had it. And I definitely shouldn't have showed it to a five-year-old. In my mind, if anyone ever found out the truth, I figured I'd spend the rest of my life behind bars."

Which is probably where you belong. But would that bring Libby back? The truth shall set you free, she thought, yet she didn't feel any freer now. If anything, she felt more imprisoned. Her best friend—killed by the stupidity of her brother. She looked up and saw the ruins of the city around her. Was it Sean's fault? Or was it more the fault of a society and culture that glorified guns and translated that down to its children? Sean said it—he felt so important. He was the man! Showing off his new toy to his little brother. And Danny... suddenly, she understood. It all made sense now. Even at five years old, he must have realized what happened. Sean probably talked to him and told him to keep quiet about it, but Danny knew. How could he have had a normal childhood after that?

"You know, more than one person died that day," she said aloud.

Sean squatted down beside her, unable to look at her. "You're right.," he murmured. "I know it killed you, and I know it killed Danny as well. I didn't know what to do after that. Danny changed. He started following me everywhere. I couldn't get rid of him."

Sean stood up and paced. "He got a taste of what guns could do, but he didn't understand it. Over and over, I wished I could've talked to him about it, but people were always around, and I didn't want anybody overhearing us. All I could do was tell him to keep his mouth shut about it. Then, as time went by, he withdrew, and it got harder and harder to talk to him. I was so angry at him, but I was even more angry at myself and it came out as angry at everyone around me, so I left. I'm sorry for it all, Em. Truly I am. If there was a way to turn the clock back, I'd do it. As for Danny, it was all a game to him. Maybe it still is."

"What do you mean? Where's Danny now?"

"I'm not sure." He looked away, and Em could see he knew more than he was telling her. She waited for him to continue. He fidgeted for a moment before speaking again. "From what I hear, he's out there now, peddlin' ghost guns to kids. A very lucrative business for him, if the reports are correct."

Em clenched her fists, struggling to contain her anger. This was fresh news to her. She didn't realize Danny still had ties to Gloomsbury, though she remembered how tight he and Sean were during her teenage years. They were always together. She had always thought Sean pushed that on Danny, but now she realized it was the other way around. Danny got caught up in it more than anyone. He tasted power at a very young age. It was when he learned what a gun could do. And more important, what it could do in *his* hand.

"You know, Danny should've graduated from high school a few months ago," she said. "Ma called me in tears and asked me if I'd come home to be with her for that weekend. She doesn't know if he's even still alive."

"Oh, he's definitely alive. Goes by the name of Danno. Everyone in the neighborhood knows him. Maybe he'd be willing to talk to you. I could try to set up a meeting. Maybe you could explain a few things to him."

She stood and looked him squarely in the face. "Maybe I could explain a few things? Why me? What makes you think he'd listen to me? You're the one who screwed us all over! If anyone should explain things to him, it's you! You're the one who gave him a gun!"

Sean looked at her helplessly. "I've tried! He wants nothing to do with me."

"Then I'm sure he'll want nothing to do with me as well. Don't talk to me about being sorry! You tore our family apart—you tore me apart—then you disappeared and left us all to figure out how to repair our broken lives, when we didn't even know what broke us to begin with."

"It's the culture here," he mumbled, looking down at the ground.

"What?" she asked.

"Everyone here has a gun. It's jus' the way it is in this city. At fourteen years old, I got caught up in that culture, and I admit, I was stupid. But it's what everyone did! Owning a gun was the only way to show you were somebody. You had power. You had status. I was desperate for that. And so was Danny. As I recall, you called him a wimp that day."

"What? I don't remember that."

"I do. I remember every minute of that day in excruciating detail. You and Libby were playin' at Libby's house, and Danny was with you. Then you came back home, and Danny was all upset 'cause he got scared of somethin' and you called him a wimp. I dunno what spooked him, but he was sure upset."

Em flinched. A vague memory jiggled in her mind. She pushed it aside. "How'd you get that gun, anyway?" she asked. "And what did you do with it after?"

"It was easy to get. Still is, I reckon. It was a 'ghost gun'—one of those shipped here in pieces and assembled here in this very city. They've had quite an operation going on for about fourteen years now. Us teenagers in the neighborhood were the guinea pigs. They wanted to start slow and then build up their market. They practically pushed those guns onto us. If you had just a little money, you could get an unregistered gun, no questions asked."

"And they're still doing that?" Em asked, dumbfounded.

"Absolutely, and on a much bigger scale, now," he said. "There's a huge underground market for them. And your little brother is at the center of it."

Em shook her head. She knew it was the culture. Ever since her first video game session with Henry, she knew this went on in neighborhoods all over the country. Still, the fact that a fourteen-year-old could easily get a gun, and indeed had guns "pushed on him" as Sean said, was unfathomable to her, and the idea of a five-year-old getting hold of a gun made her physically sick. The enormity of the problem was staggering. How could she possibly make a dent in solving this? Somewhere along the line, she had promised Libby she would be her voice, but now she simply felt helpless. What good was one voice in the face of an entire culture based on greed and violence?

8

After leaving Sean, Em wandered aimlessly through the streets as old memories assailed her. *"Who names a place Gloomsbury?"* she recalled asking her mom, about a year after they had moved out. She was in fifth grade, and one of the vocabulary words for the week had been "gloom". She had to provide three synonyms and write three sentences using that word. Sadness, depression, misery... these were all synonyms. Until then, Em hadn't known what the word meant. It was simply the name of the place where she'd grown up. One of her sentences was "I grew up in Gloomsbury." Her teacher had marked it wrong.

Her mom gave her a wan smile. Sometimes her 11-year-old daughter seemed too bright for her own good. "It's just the name of some rich white guy who wanted a someplace named after himself. It has no more meaning than that."

Em wasn't convinced. To her, words had meaning. Building a city and calling it Gloomsbury was asking for trouble. How could anyone be proud of coming from a place with that name? She sure wasn't, and she'd done everything in her power to divorce herself from that heritage. She had deliberately let the memories fade away until they became part of a different lifetime.

Now, she shuffled on leaden feet, her eyes fixed on the ground, yet some part of her felt pulled by an invisible thread. She didn't dare look up until she was standing directly in front of what used to be a house. Libby's house. Trembling, she stared across the overgrown lawn at the shell of the house, which had stood empty for many years. Fourteen years, to be exact. It looked as if Libby's family had moved out, allowing stray cats, rats, and cockroaches to move in. Trees and shrubs would have overtaken an abandoned house in the suburbs, but here in the city of Gloomsbury, the only plant life to take root was some ivy crawling up one of the side walls. One side of the roof had caved in, the siding had peeling paint, and almost all the windows were shattered, with glass shards jutting inward like jagged fangs. Glass crystals glinted all over the ground. Her gaze moved up to the one intact window. With a shudder, she realized it was the window to what had been Libby's room. For an instant, she thought she saw Libby peeking at her through the pane of glass. In that moment, she heard a now-familiar voice in her head:

***

Libby: *Thanks for coming back here.*

Em: *I didn't really have a choice. My feet took me here*

Libby: *You should buy this place.*

Em: *What?*

Libby: *Buy this house and come live here! Get a job with the local paper and be my voice!*

Em: *Be your voice? Gun control is too big a problem, Libby! I can't take on the entire National Rifle Association.*

Libby: *Maybe not, but you can take on the ghost gun industry in Gloomsbury. I will help you. You need to do this, Em!*

Em: *You expect me to end gun violence here? That's impossible!*

Libby: *I expect you to change the culture so there is no room for gun violence. To strip away the glorification of weapons for teens. There is corruption here, and you are the perfect person to uncover it. That is definitely possible.*

Em: *How?*

Em waited for an answer and none came. She blinked, and the image in the window was gone. She rubbed her eyes. What the hell was she doing, talking to a girl who died years ago? It was a stupid idea to come here. What had she hoped to accomplish?

She should leave and never return. She turned away from the skeleton of the house and walked down the street, but then stopped to look back.

What happened to the people who used to live here? There had been a kind, elderly lady with older children who sometimes babysat for Libby when her mom was working. That house was next door to Libby's and well kept up, with a fresh coat of blue paint and a neat little flower garden in the side yard. Most of the other houses were in varying stages of disrepair, but they all looked occupied. Em wondered what the neighbors thought of having such an atrocity in the middle of their neighborhood. She sighed as she turned away and continued down the street. Around the corner, she noticed the old ice cream shop was still there. Maybe she should treat herself to a cone. Her jaw dropped when the woman behind the counter stood and called her by name.

"Well, I'll be! Are you Emiline Jackson? I haven't seen the likes of you in years! What brings you back to this neck of the woods?"

Em squirmed under the woman's gaze, wishing she could run back out the door. She didn't belong here. She hadn't thought it possible anyone from her past would still be here, let alone recognize her. The woman was heavy-set and looked to be about six or seven years older than her. Em tried to place her, but her mind was blank. "I was... visiting my brother, Sean, and wanted to see this old neighborhood. Sean works just a few blocks from here, at the auto-body shop. I just started wandering and found myself here...."

"You don't recognize me, do you? I'm Sarah Williamson. My mom used to watch you and Libby sometimes. Mom passed away a few years ago, but I live in the house next door to..."

"You mean the house with the garden? It's beautiful!"

"Thank you. We do what we can to keep the neighborhood looking decent, but with that... eyesore there, it's challenging. For years, we've been trying to get that house torn down, but it's been tied up in land court. The family left, but for some reason, the city won't release the land." She leaned in toward Em and whispered, "The place is haunted, you know."

Em forced a weak smile. Talking about Libby's house like this made her uncomfortable. Somehow, it felt like gossip. She wondered how often the neighbors would look at that house and shake their heads in resignation. Did they think bad thoughts about Libby's family for abandoning the property? Sarah kept talking. "They say no one will go in there now, ever. But I don't know... every once in a while, I hear things. Men's voices, mostly. It's spooky, alright."

Tell her! Libby's voice again. Em hesitated, then blurted out, "I'm thinking of buying it!"

"What?" Sarah exclaimed. "You must be outta your mind! First, I don't think it's even for sale, and second, what in God's name would you do with it? Surely, you don't think you would live there?"

"I don't know," Em mumbled. "Today, I just found myself here, standing in front of that house, and felt a powerful tug to own it. I've been living in Washington, D.C., and I'm ready for a change. Do you know anyone I could talk to if I wanted to buy it?"

"You can't be serious!" Sarah said, shaking her head. "You're askin' for trouble. But if you really want to pursue this, call my brother Joey. He's a realtor." She scribbled a phone number and handed it to Em. " I'm sure he'll tell you the same thing I did, but at least you can say you tried. And since you're here... can I treat you to some ice cream? We have many of the same flavors you might remember from years ago!"

"Thanks," Em said. As Sarah turned to get her ice cream, she realized how much smaller the shop seemed than when she'd been a kid. There was a copy of *The Gloomsbury Post* on the top shelf of a newspaper rack in the corner. She picked it up and browsed the few pages. Libby's voice echoed in her head: *Get a job with the local paper and be my voice!*

"Is this the only local paper?" she asked.

"Yeah," replied Sarah. "Sadly, it's the best thing we have. It only costs 25 cents and I'm not sure it's even worth that. I wish there were more local stories. Rumor has it the owner is afraid of publishing anything controversial and most things in this city worth reporting fall into that category. So, they just write about school happenings, bus routes, sports, weddings, that kind of stuff. There's a police and fire log, but I'm not sure how complete it is. Not really news if you ask me, but nothing the editor might get a death threat about either."

"Do you know the editor?" Em asked. "If I end up moving here, I'll need a job, and I'd love to write for the local paper, even part-time."

"Sure! I know everyone around here. His name is Samuel Brighton, and he's a crotchety old man," replied Sarah. "I'll introduce you, though I don't know how open he'll be to new ideas. The office is just a few blocks from here. Let me call and see if he has time to talk to you."

***

Em stared at the sign outside the building: THE GLOOMSBURY POST. It certainly looked imposing. She hoped Mr. Brighton would be in a good mood and willing to listen to her proposal. Squaring her shoulders, she rang the buzzer. So far today, Libby seemed to have orchestrated everything. She took a deep breath and hoped Libby wouldn't desert her now.

A gruff-looking black man opened the door a crack, then beckoned her in. Em looked around the bare room. Two desks sat in the middle with two computers and a printer, while eight file cabinets lined the walls. Despite its lack of other furnishings, the room was well-lit and looked like an efficient workspace.

"Thank you for seeing me on such short notice," she said.

"Well, Sarah's a good friend, and I like to do favors for my friends. She says you may be looking for a job. I don't need any full-time workers right now. Couldn't afford to pay you even if I needed the work done. But she seemed to think you might be interested in something part-time."

"I've been a reporter for the *Post* in Washington for the last two years. Mostly I wrote about fashion and restaurants... things of interest to city folk. I could do something like that for your paper. I noticed you have little in the way of profiling local businesses."

He raised his eyebrows. "You're right... we don't do much of that. I haven't had anyone to write that since the last reporter resigned. Like I said, I can't afford to pay a full-time reporter to write that kind of stuff."

"Well, I could write some of that part-time. But what I really want to do is offer you a trade."

"A trade?"

Em fidgeted, but forged ahead, feeling as if she was on autopilot. "Yes. You see, I grew up in this city and my family moved away because of all the gun violence that was going on.

I'd like to return here and do something to make Gloomsbury a safer place. I want to start up an organization, but need help to publicize it. If I could use your paper as a platform, I could get the word out to people. I'd be willing to write some stories about local businesses for free, if you would also publish some short articles about my organization."

He narrowed his eyes. "What is this organization you're talking about?"

She took a deep breath. It felt like she was jumping off a cliff. Though she had been thinking about this for a while, she had yet to verbalize it to anyone—even Cara. "It's called "GHOST" which stands for "Guns Hurt Our Souls, Too." I want to eliminate the sale of ghost guns in Gloomsbury, and to do that, I need broad support from the community. I'm looking to educate people about the problem and see if together we can come up with some solutions that will improve life here."

"So you want to write articles for the paper highlighting local businesses, and have me publish some things you've also written about your personal business?"

"More or less... though it's not exactly my personal business. It's more like a cause I'm involved in..." She felt like she was floundering.

"I must say, this is a most unusual request. I'll have to think on it. In the meantime, send me some things you've written for your previous paper, and a sample of what you might want to write about this Ghost thing."

Em's face lit up. "I really appreciate you considering this! I know it's strange, but it can't be any stranger than the day I've had today!"

9

The door groaned, and the floorboard creaked under her feet. "What do you all think?" Em asked, stepping into the house. She looked back at Cara, Ron, and Henry with trepidation. As the excitement of buying the house wore off and reality sank in, she wondered if it was a good idea. She needed the affirmation of her friends. "Um... the house has good bones," Ron offered. "A lot of time and money could make it livable..."

Cara nudged him. "It's amazing, Em! We can fix it up. Ron's right—it'll take a lot of effort, but we'll help you. It'll be a fun project!"

"You really think so?" Em looked around at the peeling paint, ripped curtains, and dusty, dirty windows. The radiator in the corner let out a loud hiss, causing her to jump. "I wonder if the water works." She moved into the kitchen and turned on the faucet. A gray stream of water spurted out.

"A good cleaning and a few coats of paint will make a world of difference," said Henry. "I think you should go for it. After all, you said the price is right."

"The price is next to nothing, but city officials want it torn down. The thing is... I don't want to tear it down. It's the house, not the land I'm interested in. I want to live in this house, but if I intend to fix it up, the building inspector needs to know I have the resources and support to do that. Ron, can you help me come up with a plan?"

Ron nodded. "I have a little experience with house renovation. You should have seen my house when we bought it. It wasn't quite like this, but it needed a lot of work. Sure, I'll help. But first, I want to hear more about the rumors that it's haunted."

"Did you say 'haunted'?" asked Henry.

As if on cue, the door creaked opened and Sarah Williamson poked her head in. "Sorry to barge in like this, but my brother Joey told me you'd be here lookin' at the house today. I can't believe you're really serious about buying it. Figured I'd come by and see if I can answer any questions."

"Hi Sarah," Em said. "These are my friends, Cara, Ron and Henry. They're the ones who can help me fix this place up." Turning to her friends, she added, "Sarah lives next door in the house with the gorgeous garden. And she owns the ice cream shop down the street."

Cara held out her hand. "Pleased to meet you, Sarah. Your garden is magnificent."

"I don't know if it's magnificent, but we do what we can to create a little beauty around here," she said modestly. "You fix this place up, though, and it'll do a world of good for the neighborhood. We need some fresh energy around here."

"How safe is it here?" asked Cara.

Sarah laughed bitterly. "Safe? Ain't no place safe around here. We just have to live smart, is all. These young kids come into my shop and they ain't bad kids... they just have bad toys. You have to find the things that motivate them. Ice cream, for one. They know I won't serve 'em if they're carrying guns. I tell 'em 'fine—go ahead and shoot me if you want. Put me out of my misery.' But then I tell 'em I'll come back from beyond the grave and haunt 'em. I tell them I'll make sure they spend the rest of their miserable lives in jail with no ice cream. That usually gets their attention."

"I'm making an offer to buy it!" Em announced. "And I'm not tearing it down. Haunted or not, I'm going to live here and make some positive changes to this neighborhood."

"That's the second time you've said the house is haunted," said Henry. "What's the deal with that?"

Em opened her mouth to reply, but Sarah cut in. "It's haunted alright. I sometimes hear the voices late at night."

"Maybe it's just kids using this house for drug deals," Ron offered. Cara glared at him, but he shrugged. "An abandoned house would be the perfect place for something like that."

"Maybe," Sarah admitted. "But most of the kids around here are terrified of this place. They're the ones who say it's haunted. They won't go near it. I've seen 'em playin' chicken around here. They dare each other to approach the door. And, unfortunately, I've seen 'em throwing rocks through the windows." She strode to one of the broken windows and picked up a fist-sized stone. "Like this one here."

"Well, all that will change because I'm going to move in here and make this place beautiful. If they continue to throw rocks through the windows, they'll risk getting arrested."

"Best of luck to you, then," said Sarah. "I'm rootin' for you, but don't get your hopes too high. Change takes time, you know."

***

To Em's surprise. Henry called her the next day.

"I'll get right to the point," he said. "If you're serious about moving into that house, you need to learn to use a gun. For self-defense."

"I don't think so," she replied tersely. "That's just buying into the whole idea that it's the culture there."

"It *is* the culture there. That's exactly the issue. If you want to fit into that culture, at least learn the things those kids have learned. It's like learning their language."

"I already learned their language! All those video games you showed me... isn't that the language they speak?"

"That's like elementary school and middle school," he said. "You need to move on to high school now. To see what shooting a real gun actually feels like."

Em shuddered. She didn't want to take this step, but it was part of the deal she'd made with Henry. "Okay," she said. "One lesson, if you promise to help me with house renovations. But I'm not planning to purchase a gun for self-defense."

"I'm happy to help you with the house. Especially if Cara and Ron will be there." he said.

The following morning, Em stood in front of the barn-like building that was part of the gun range. In the distance, she heard the muffled sound of gunfire. She followed Henry inside and watched while he carefully laid all their equipment on a table.

"None of this is dangerous. These are all dummy cartridges. We'll talk about gun safety in here, then go outside to do some shooting," he said.

"They don't do any background checks here or anything?"

"Nah," he said. "I'm a member of the club, and all members need a valid license to carry. There were a few tests I had to take as well. I can bring in anyone I want as a guest as long as I'm supervising them the whole time. Believe me, you're safer here than anywhere else in this city. This is a place for people to learn about gun safety and enjoy themselves. Unfortunately, most teenagers in inner cities and poverty-stricken districts don't get this kind of instruction. That's something you may want to focus on in your writing."

Henry systematically showed her the parts of the gun and talked about safety before taking her outside.

Pop-pop-pop. The sounds struck her immediately. Henry handed her earmuffs. "Mid-morning on a weekday is the best time of day to come," he explained. "It can get crowded later in the day and be overwhelming and noisy. There's more to learn before you can shoot."

Henry showed her how to stand and how to hold the pistol. It was unloaded at first, and after his demo, he put it down, then stood back and motioned for her to pick it up. "Never hand a gun to someone. You take your turn, then put it on the table and let the other person pick it up." Gingerly, she took it with her fingertips. The lightness of it surprised her.

"Go ahead and hold it," he urged. "The gun by itself can't hurt you. It's the human operators you need to be worried about. This is what I meant when I told you: guns aren't the issue, people are."

"It feels like it's made of plastic!" she exclaimed. "How can something this light be so dangerous?"

"Many of the newer guns are plastic. In fact, they can make most of the parts in a 3-D printer. This is what's often market-ed to kids these days. This is a semi-automatic pistol. It's small, lightweight, and feels almost like a toy. I'm sure you're not the only one questioning how these can be so deadly. Remember the video games? This makes the translation from gaming to reality easier. You'll definitely notice a kickback when you fire it though."

He had her pick the pistol up a few times, then showed her how to load the ammunition. When he fired, she flinched, assaulted by both the sound and the smell of gunpowder. She closed her eyes briefly, grateful for the ear protection. The sound of gunfire was one that she knew she had to get used to if she was going to live in Libby's house. She made a mental note to purchase some high-quality earmuffs. But the smell... she didn't know if she'd ever be able to get used to that.

Henry fired off a few rounds, then unloaded the gun and placed it back on the table. "Your turn," he said. She worked slowly, methodically sliding the magazine into the grip, as he had shown her. Trembling, she aimed at the target and pulled the trigger. She jumped at the recoil in her hand. The bullet went wide, and the empty casing fell to the ground. She looked around, noticing the ground was littered with empty brass.

"First rule, and I know it's a tough one. Keep both eyes open and on the target. Think of it as playing tennis. You need to keep your eye on the ball, right?"

"Right, but that's a moving target. This one's just sitting there," she said.

"True, but as you get more advanced, you may try shooting at targets that are moving. Better to not develop a habit of squeezing your eyes closed."

She nodded and tried again. This time, the bullet grazed the target. A few more times, and she was hitting it with more consistency.

"Relax your shoulders," Henry advised. "Let them sink down, away from your ears."

She tried again and hit closer to the center. This was proving to be less of an ordeal than she had expected. Once again, she could see how kids could be drawn to this. If she hadn't once witnessed how easily guns could kill, she could almost admit she was having fun. That thought made her want to cut the session short.

"I think I'm done here," she said, placing the gun back on the table. "You're right... it has been eye-opening."

"We can stop now. But first, I want you to experience it without ear protection. It's really different," he said.

She removed the earmuffs and watched as Henry fired one bullet. The sound sent her reeling. Her dream had always been silent, but the sound of the single shot propelled her back in time. She doubled over, clutching at her belly as she recalled Libby lying on the driveway. For a moment, she thought she might be physically sick. In the distance, she heard more loud shots as other people practiced on the range. She straightened up and fumbled to put her earmuffs back on. The distant sounds were not nearly as bad when muffled.

"In that part of the city, you will need to be prepared for the sounds of gunfire. I'm not saying it will happen, but it might. At least now, it won't surprise you. And I know you may resist this, but at least think about getting a permit and buying a small pistol to keep in your house, in case you need it for self-defense. I can help you with that if you want," said Henry.

Her shoulders slumped. Part of her wanted to scream, "NO!" yet another part felt he might be right. What was she getting herself into by moving into that house?

10

Em looked around her apartment at all the stuff she planned to take to her new house. For the past six months, she had been busy renovating the house. Moving day was now a week away, yet instead of packing, she had been putting her effort into making a splash when she arrived in the city. Her idea of creating an online magazine as a platform to write about gun violence had changed since she'd bought the house and spoken with Samuel Brighton, the editor of the *Gloomsbury Post*. Libby's words replayed in her head: *"Maybe you can't take on the whole NRA, but you can take on the ghost gun industry in Gloomsbury."*

She intended to start a GHOST movement in the city, and thought the best way to publicize that would be through a physical, local paper. Keeping the pen name of Libby, she planned to write a brief article each week. Hopefully, the right people would come forward and be her allies. She had already sent Samuel a few articles she'd written about local businesses in Washington, and she had done a write-up of Sarah's ice cream shop, which both Samuel and Sarah loved. Added to that, her first article about GHOST was now ready to go. She looked it over one more time.

From The Gloomsbury Post Ghost

Here in Gloomsbury, we live in a state of terror and perpetual fear. People are afraid to venture from their homes. Any moment, we could be hit by a stray bullet—or one meant for us because we offended someone. What kind of life is this? This epidemic needs to be stopped. I intend to stop it.

Who am I? I am Libby, The Ghost of Gloomsbury.

Who am I, really? My name was Libby, and I am no longer alive. Years ago, a five-year-old boy, who should never have had a gun in his hand, shot and killed me.

You may ask: *What was a five-year-old doing with a gun?* It was a ghost gun belonging to his fourteen-year-old brother, who also should never have had a gun, yet he bought it easily. Ghost guns, along with the organized effort to sell them to teenagers, have fueled gang violence, changed the landscape of this city, and ended my life. Yet my spirit has remained trapped in my house ever since.

I could haunt your thoughts, but it's really these guns that haunt you. The culture here needs to shift. Get ghost guns off the streets and out of the hands of children! If you don't, all that will be left of your city will be a collection of restless spirits. What can you do about it?

Join GHOST:
A grassroots organization dedicated to eliminating ghost guns

GHOST: Guns Hurt Our Souls, Too.
To join me in this fight, send me your name and contact information.

Satisfied, she added her address (a brand-new P.O. box number) and put it aside. Perhaps no one would respond, and she was completely out of her mind to tackle this, but she had to try. *Gloomsbury, here I come!* The thought both terrified and excited her.

Two days later, Samuel Brighton emailed her that her first article about Sarah's shop, along with her promotion of GHOST, would be in the paper the following day.

***

When she went to the house the following morning to bring over a few boxes of items she didn't trust the movers to handle, she found a note taped to her front door, written in child-like script. Her stomach rolled as she realized who it was from.

Dear Em –

I hear you moving back to town. I'm not sure this is a good idea for you. I want to talk to you about it. Meet me in the park near our old house. Remember the swing set we used to play on? Meet me there tomorrow 10:00 am.

Your brother, Danno

Danno? That was the name Sean said Danny now used. How did he know she was here? The article had appeared in the paper that morning, but she had deliberately left her name off it. No one else in the city besides Sarah knew she was buying this house. Then again, Danny was the one who shot Libby. It wouldn't take much for him to connect the dots. Would it be dangerous to meet with him alone? She thought of the gun she had recently bought at Henry's urging. Following his advice, she had done a certification class and gotten a gun permit along with a small pistol, though she couldn't imagine ever using it. It sat in a drawer of her bedside table. She shook the thought of bringing it with her aside. This was her brother, after all. She shouldn't be afraid to meet with him in a public park. Carrying a gun for self-defense wouldn't make her any safer.

Now, as she approached the park, she thought she should have at least brought a friend. Confusion showed on her face as she tried to reconcile the young child of her memory with the 19-year-old man casually sitting on the swing. He was full-grown, and though he had a smaller build than Sean, he looked a little beefier. Like Sean, his skin was coal-black, just as she had remembered. The moustache and beard certainly added to his mystique. He carried himself with confidence.

"Well, well, well. If it ain't my big sister comin' to pay a visit," he said.

"Hello, Danny," she said, taking a seat on the swing next to him. "It's been a long time."

"That it has," he acknowledged. "That it has. You ain't changed much, though. I'd recognize you anywhere."

Em was thrown off guard. Her brother Sean, her neighbor Sarah, and now Danny, all had said they recognized her from her childhood. Yet she felt the child who grew up here was a different person. Did she really still look the same? She turned her attention back to Danny, who was asking her a pointed question.

"I hear you're movin' into town soon. Is that true?" Em nodded. "Why?" he pressed.

"I grew up here. What's it matter to you?"

"It matters a lot when you go writin' this stuff in the local paper." He held up a copy of the newspaper. "Why you tryin' to change things around here? You come in with all your high-falutin' ideas about how things should be here. Your way. But what if we like it our way? Maybe we like it like this."

"What, the poverty? The filth? The violence that happens every day? Look around. How could you possibly like this?"

"I like my freedom and the fact I can make some good money."

"What you like is the sense of power and control you have. But that comes at a cost of other people's misery."

"You know nothing about misery and what I like or don't like. Listen, I know everythin' that happens around here. I could have you eliminated if I want. The only reason you's still alive is because you're my sister. When I heard you were movin' in, I gave you special protective status. I wanted to see what you were up to. But now, I could have that protection taken away...." His eyes turned steely. "You interfering with my business. That's not good E. Not good at all. You need to stop."

"Stop?" She glared at him.

"Yeah, stop your lobbyin'. Stop tryin' to change things around here. It's bad for business—*my* business."

"You really think you're a king," she said softly.

"Actually, I *know* I'm King. At least in this little slice of the city. What I say goes, and I'm telling you now... you need to go. Or rather, just don't move in."

"What're you going to do, shoot me?" she challenged. "Will that make you happy? I don't think so. You killed my best friend. You stole her soul. And so, no, I am not going away. Not until your kingdom is destroyed. This is war, Danny, and I intend to win."

"Stole your friend's soul?" He spat on the ground. "What you talkin' about? She was jus' in the wrong place. I didn' mean to kill her, but, you know, shit happens."

"Are you telling me you're not at all sorry? That you feel nothing about taking the life of a 10-year-old girl?"

"What should I feel? It wasn't my fault! Blame Sean if you want to blame someone. I didn't know what I was doing. But once it happened, I learned somethin'."

"What did you learn, Danny?"

"I learned guns rule around here, and those who aren't afraid to use them are the ones who thrive."

"Is that all you learned?"

He shrugged. "What else should I have learned? That I'm not a wimp?"

Em flinched as a fuzzy memory once again tried to surface. Hadn't Sean said something similar? She shook off that thought, unable to believe her brother could think this way. Was he trying to put the blame on her? She struggled to remind herself he had only been five years old when this happened, and there had been no consequences for him. No one else besides

Sean knew who fired the gun and what really happened. Their family had moved and never spoke of it again.

"Maybe you should have learned that once a person dies, they are gone forever," she spat back at him. "That every life is precious. That guns have no place in the hands of children. But here you are, telling me you are profiting from making it easy for kids to kill. You told me to stop, Danny, but I won't until the ghost gun industry in this city is destroyed. I don't care about your business and I don't care about you. Your days as a king are over. Don't bother me again. That house is my home now, and I intend to stay there for a long time."

She stormed off, knowing the battle lines had been drawn.

11

It was her third morning in her new house. In that semi-awake state between sleep and waking, Em heard gunfire outside, and somewhere beyond that sound she heard Libby's voice. Sarah's conviction that the house was haunted gave her pause. Was it possible Libby's ghost was actually talking to her? Or was this simply that voice in her head she thought of as her other identity? Did it even matter?

Libby: *Why'd you move here?*

Em: *I moved here to stop gun violence in this city.*

Libby: *Right, but did you have a plan how to do that? You need to gain some perspective first and see there are many ways to look at this. Your brother is just a small piece of this. What have you learned so far?*

Em closed her eyes. What had she learned since moving here?

Em: *I guess I've learned the roots of violence and hatred run far deeper than I ever imagined. And I'm powerless to fix it.*

Libby: *Well, you got part of it right. The roots do go deep. But the part about fixing it... why do you keep thinking you are powerless?*

Em: *I don't know where to start. Who am I to think I can fix this? Is it even my problem to solve?*

Libby: *If you're not fighting for yourself, then who are you fighting for?*

Em: *For you and all those others who died by violence. And also for the loved ones they left behind.*

Libby: *So... gather your forces! There are many out there who will join you in this fight. Find them.*

***

Em opened her laptop and wrote:

From The Gloomsbury Post Ghost

I woke up this morning to the sound of gunfire for the third day in a row. The front window, replaced just before I moved last week, shattered on the ground floor of my house. Is someone trying to scare me away? It's July... it's hot, and I'm told this spate of violence will last until the heat subsides. No—I don't live in a war zone. I live in a house haunted by my friend Libby, who died here years ago. I was with her when she was shot, and

this house is in *your city*, where gang violence has been the norm for years.

"It's the culture here," my older brother told me. "It'll never change." Maybe he's right. Maybe that's true, but I intend to change it. For too long, we have ignored it, put up with it, treated it like it wasn't our problem. But it is our problem. I moved back here to understand it, to live with it and bring that understanding to you all. The roots of gun violence start here—in the inner cities and towns where poverty flourishes and hatred breeds. What are *we* going to do about it?

Libby is no longer alive, but I will write for her and as her until I don't need to anymore. When guns no longer rule here, her soul can finally rest. Until then, I'm asking you to get educated and to join me in my campaign to end this scourge of guns here in Gloomsbury.

Remember: GHOST: Guns Hurt Our Souls, Too

***

The day after the second article about GHOST came out, Em found herself in Sarah's kitchen, bemoaning her decision to buy the house.

"I know it's my brother trying to scare me away. I don't want to give in, but I don't know if I can survive this," she confided in her neighbor.

"Why'd you move here, really?" asked Sarah.

"I'm not sure! When I first saw the house and how run down it was, I felt a strong connection to Libby and wanted to fix it up for her sake. I've always wanted to be her voice in some way. I want to stop the scourge of gun violence and eliminate ghost guns here, but now I wonder if that's just a pipe dream. It's too big a problem for me."

"You're right, it's a huge problem. Any one person alone can't solve it. But you don't have to do it alone, and you don't have to do it all at once. You've already done so much to the house. Even with those broken windows, it looks so much more beautiful than it did six months ago. I know the house inspector told you to tear it down, but you were right to keep it as it is. The house looks like it belongs here. Your friends are amazing for working with you. You are amazing. Remember what I told you... change doesn't happen easily or quickly."

"Thanks. I guess I'm just feeling so helpless. And scared. The sound of gunshots has brought back more childhood memories. I heard them when my family lived here, but never after we moved away. I blocked all that out of my mind. When Henry took me to the shooting range, I realized the sound would remind me of Libby's death, but it's brought up more than that. I remember feeling scared even as a very young child. How do you deal with it, day after day?"

"It becomes part of the background of your life. After a while, you don't notice it as much. Truth be told, the noises I used to hear comin' from that house bothered me more. I told you I thought it was haunted, and that may be true. But I also wonder if there were kids goin' in there and using the house for things... like storing stuff there. Maybe that's why they want you out. Maybe there's somethin' in there they need."

Em shook her head. "I've fully renovated the house and cleaned every inch. If there was anything there, we would have found it. I think Danny's just trying to scare me away because I'm bad for his business. There must be a way to reach him. I can't believe he's grown into this."

"He's a product of his environment, Em," said Sarah. "You may not be able to change that."

"I grew up here. How did I not know it was like this? How have I ignored this my entire adult life?"

"You weren't ready to face it. But now you are."

"What can I possibly do? It feels too big."

"Why not hold a vigil?" asked Sarah.

"A vigil? What do you mean?"

"You're building a following with your Post Ghost, or whatever it is you call it. You told me you've had a bunch of people call and email you to sign up. Why not do something for them? Have a gathering of people who've lost someone to gun violence. Here in Gloomsbury there's a huge number of folk in that category. Have people come and honor their loved ones publicly. Make it an event."

"Maybe, but would it be safe?"

"Well, you'd have to talk to the police to see about getting protection for the event. Then get a permit from the city for where you're going to do it. I like the idea of the old Town Common. There's a big open space there. Ask everyone to bring a flower in their loved one's memory, and then give people a chance to speak if they want."

Sarah paused for a moment, then snapped her fingers. "You know, it's getting close to Halloween. In Detroit and other big cities, there was a tradition called 'Devil's Night' before Halloween when people would run around starting fires and destroying things. I heard it's being replaced by 'Angel's Night.' How about we start something here called 'Spirit's Night' or 'Ghost's Night' and use this vigil to promote it? Let Libby come out in force, and maybe some other spirits will choose to join in with her!"

Em looked at Sarah with wonder. She had thought no one else truly believed in the existence of Libby as a spirit, but she could see how Sarah was sold on the idea. Perhaps others would be as well.

"I'll think about it," she replied. "You're right that I'm building a following and lots of people are contacting me. Maybe I'll talk to the police about organizing this. It can't hurt, right?"

***

From The Gloomsbury Post Ghost

Here's what Libby told me last night:

"Gloomsbury is a wasteland. A ghost town. Spirits walk the streets. Too many deaths. Too much violence. How will it end?"

"Isn't it odd that people say 'Rest in Peace' at a funeral? You may sleep at night, but spirits don't. A spirit can never rest in peace if someone has yanked it out of this world in a violent way... until that violence is dissolved. Illegal ghost guns are a scourge on this city, preventing me and hundreds of spirits like me from resting in peace. Until those guns are removed, we are stuck in a strange purgatory. So... we haunt you. If we can't sleep at night, then neither should you."

I am committed to getting ghost guns off the streets. Are you with me? If so, join GHOST by sending me your name and contact information. Together, we can make a difference.

GHOST: Guns Hurt Our Souls, Too

12

Lieutenant Vance sat at his office desk twiddling his thumbs. He glanced at the single entry for the day on his calendar: Emiline Jackson. She had emailed him the day before asking if she could talk to him about something important for the town.

Her recent move to Gloomsbury was causing a stir due to her articles in the local paper about ending gun violence. Who did she think she was? His phone buzzed, and he pressed the speaker button on his desk as he glanced at the clock. Right on time. "I'll be out in a few minutes," he said. Let her stew for a bit, he thought.

He took a bite of a jelly donut and pondered her name. *Jackson... Why was that name familiar?* And then it hit him. It was one of his first calls when he had joined the police force fourteen years ago. Girl shot in the driveway as he recalled. A drive-by shooting according to the kids who were there. Sean Jackson was the name of the kid who had called it in. Of course! Now he remembered. Sean was there with his younger sister and brother, and clearly stated he'd seen a car whiz by chasing some guy running down the street. End of story. Vance had taken the names of the three kids, and filed the report. He couldn't remember the name of the younger boy, but he was almost certain the little girl was Emiline. The family moved away shortly after that, and he never gave it another thought. What could she want from this city now? Did she seriously think she could end gun violence here?

***

Em stood in the corner of the police station lobby. It had been ten minutes. Should she approach the white, scruffy-haired clerk again? He hadn't been very welcoming when she mentioned her appointment with Lieutenant Vance. "He'll be out in a few minutes. I'd say take a seat, but there ain't much in the way of chairs here. You can just wait over there." He had motioned vaguely to the corner of the room and turned his attention to his cell phone.

The clerk sat at a desk behind a bulletproof window. The room was unfurnished, aside from his desk and chair. Under the eerie glow of a single, bare yellow lightbulb, Em glanced at a few fliers highlighting city ordinances (and the fines for disobeying them) taped haphazardly to the dull gray walls.

She wished she had asked Sarah to come with her, but shoved that thought aside. She could do this by herself. After all, the police should welcome having someone in town who cared about gun violence. The only reason they might not support this was money. It all came down to what resources the city had. The cracked paint on the walls suggested there wasn't a lot of money to spare. She hoped Lieutenant Vance would be receptive to her request for a guard to watch over a planned vigil spotlighting gun violence. She was about to ask the ragged clerk to call him again when an imposing man dressed in full uniform strode into the room.

"What can I do for you, Ma'am?"

Momentarily thrown off guard by the formal greeting, she glanced at the clerk, who remained engrossed in his cell phone. She had hoped to have a more private place to talk, but this would have to do. She studied Lieutenant Vance. He looked vaguely familiar. Was it his close-cropped hair? Or something about his eyes? She took a deep breath and nervously began a well-rehearsed speech. "My name is Emiline Jackson, and I lived here in Gloomsbury until I was 10 years old. My family left after someone shot my best friend in front of me in our driveway. They felt this was no place to raise us. I'm grateful they did that, but now I've realized I was one of the lucky ones. I got out, but many kids in this city aren't so lucky. They continue to live in a culture of violence."

He gave her a look of scorn, a wad of chewing gum in his mouth. "So, what's your point? What do you want from us?"

She took a deep breath and straightened up. "Recently, I moved back here from the Washington, D.C. area and I've started a grass-roots organization called GHOST. It stands for Guns-"

"I know what it stands for. I've seen your articles in the paper. Seems like you think you can make a difference here."

"Well, I'm not sure about that, but I have gotten some people interested. We'd like to hold a vigil to remember our loved ones who died from gun violence. We want to have a public event, and for that we need police protection."

"A vigil.... Here, in Gloomsbury? Now that's something different. Tell me more about what you're planning," he said.

At least it wasn't a flat-out "forget it." Encouraged, she continued, "We have nothing planned yet. I'm starting by talking to you. We'd like to do it soon, before Halloween. In some places, the night before Halloween has become a time of violence. It's been called 'Devil's Night' because people do all sorts of damage and mischief. Some cities, though, are turning October 30th into 'Angel's Night,' and here in Gloomsbury we'd like to designate October 30th as 'Ghost's Night', to remember all those who've died from gun violence in this city. We want to use this vigil to publicize Ghost's Night and honor those victims. Their lives mattered. Ultimately, we want to get guns—especially ghost guns—off the streets. I should think you'd want that as well."

He narrowed his eyes, and his cheeks moved in and out as he continued to chew. "What makes you think you can breeze into town and solve a problem that's plagued this city for decades?"

"I don't know if I can solve it, but for the sake of my friend, I have to try. Maybe nothing will come of this. Maybe I'll get driven out. I don't know how this will end, but I've heard from many people here in the city who are sick of this problem and want to work with me to change things."

"Okay—so you haven't told me what you're planning. How many people? Are you thinking of having a rally with speakers?"

"Not exactly," she said slowly. "We want people to bring a flower in memory of their loved one. If we do it on the old Town Common, it might be a way to make that area beautiful for a day or two. People can put down a flower and maybe say a sentence or two about the person they are honoring. I'm not sure how long people will stay—though with police protection, they may stay longer. Maybe I'll give a brief speech and we'll have a moment of silence. People can stay and gather or share stories if they want, but I don't see it as much more organized than that."

He chewed his gum some more. "Okay, here's what I can do for you, Ms. Jackson. We'd have to add a few extra patrolmen to that shift, and that costs money. We can give you a half hour of protection for four hundred dollars. Cash payment. So... you can tell all your people to come, lay down their flowers, and then leave. No loitering around, or 'gathering' as you call it. And it needs to be finished early in the evening, say 5:00 pm. I'm sure you know it isn't safe to be out on the streets in this city after dark."

As she walked out the door, Vance smirked at her, before turning to the clerk. Had she dawdled a moment longer, she would have heard him ask the clerk to dig up a fourteen-year-old file from the police archives, followed by the statement, "This vigil is a bad idea."

Though she didn't hear his words, the parting look he gave her set her on edge. She wasn't sure what to think of Lieutenant Vance and his offer. His gruff manner upset her. What could she hope to accomplish in a half hour? Would the police really provide protection, or was this just a ploy for them to get more money? She had almost one hundred followers—people who had sent her their contact information. Could she ask each person to contribute four or five dollars? Then there was the problem of how people would get home safely. Vance was right about one thing—the streets weren't safe after dark. Maybe it would be better to do this earlier in the day. She kept picturing how the event could go as she made her way to Sarah's ice cream shop, where she found herself face to face with her brother, Danny. He was holding the newspaper with her latest article in his hand.

"Didn' I tell you to stop this nonsense?" he said, waving the paper in her face.

"You did, but since when do I take orders from you?" She glared at him.

Sarah bustled over. She shook her finger at Danny. "Hold on a minute here... not in my shop! You got a beef with her, you take it far away from here."

Danny scowled at her. "I was jus' leaving anyways. Em, you better stop this or you'll be sorry." He turned and beckoned to a group of boys seated at one of tables. They all rose and scurried after him as he walked out.

"He's trouble, that one. See how the others follow his orders?" Sarah said. "I don't think he'd do anything to you directly, but he might get one of his lackeys to do the dirty work. You're causing a big stir in town, and it's high time, I say. Just be careful around him, Em."

"He makes me so angry! I came in here to talk to you about this vigil—I had all sorts of doubts about whether I could really pull it off, but after seeing him right now, I'm more resolved than ever to do it. I need your help, Sarah. Do you think we can raise four hundred dollars? Would people pay four dollars each to do something like this?"

"Of course! They pay three dollars for an ice cream cone! Don't be afraid to ask for donations. I'm tellin' you—most people in this city want guns off the streets. No one, except those kids who follow him like puppy dogs, likes what your brother is doin'."

13

From The Gloomsbuury Post Ghost

Join the
GHOST VIGIL
to honor the memories of those lost to gun violence in this city

Sunday, October 1 from 3:00 to 3:30 pm

Bring a flower to beautify the Old Town Common
A donation of $4.00 per victim is requested to cover the cost of police protection

In any other city or town, asking private citizens to donate money for extra police protection at a public event would sound crazy. Why should private citizens have to pay to get a police detail for a public event? But Glooms-

bury isn't any other city. Given the city's resources, this is what it takes to hold a safe vigil. We need YOU to be part of it. Be there if you care about ending gun violence in Gloomsbury! Let your voices ring.

***

The afternoon of October 1st was cool and drizzly. Em stood on the Common, watching family after family lay down flowers and deposit money into the cash box. She had expected seventy to eighty people based on responses she'd received, but already by 3:15 pm, well over three hundred people had shown up. Em and Sarah had marked off a walking path with space on either side for flowers, and a tall black woman from the crowd was overseeing the flower placement.

"That's Isabella Higgins," said Sarah. "She owns the flower shop across town, where I get the flowers to keep my house lookin' beautiful. I asked her to come and help arrange things here when I heard how busy her shop was the past two days. As a prominent business owner here in the city, she's prob'ly a good person to have on your team. Her husband, Charles, is a fourth-grade teacher and the only black person on the city council. He often clashes with the rest of the councilors, and I hear some of their meetings have been pretty heated. If we don't have time to talk to her today, I'll introduce you to her this week." Em nodded as she watched Isabella expertly direct people where to place their flowers.

"You should be right proud of yourself," Sarah continued. "Look at all the people! There hasn't been a gathering this size in Gloomsbury for years! People have been too afraid to venture out."

"I know. I wish everyone could stay longer."

"It's just the beginning," replied Sarah. "Remember... baby steps. Get up there now and let people know why you asked them to come today."

Lieutenant Vance stood on the perimeter and she felt his agitation as people continued to pour in. She needed to speak now, before the police started forcing people to leave.

She stood at the makeshift podium and picked up the megaphone Sarah had brought. "Good afternoon!" her voice boomed out over the Common. People stopped talking and turned to her. Many were crying. She looked at the sea of people around her—people of all ages, united by a common cause.

"My name is Emiline Jackson, and I am glad so many of you are here today. This morning, I looked at the weather forecast, and worried the rain might keep people away. We have a lot more people than I expected, so I don't think that's the case. In fact, I think the rain is appropriate. The heavens are crying with us. Today is a time to grieve the loss of our loved ones, to remember them, and to resolve to move forward so others don't suffer as we have. We are here to make a statement. For too long, violence has plagued Gloomsbury, and it's time for that to end. Let's pause for a moment of silence." Em bowed her head and said a quick prayer to Libby. *Thank you for pushing me. I know you are with me on this.* Libby's response was immediate. *Always...*

Em continued, "Gloomsbury, this is just the beginning. The ghosts and spirits of all those whose lives were cut short by guns are with us. The air is thick with them. You can feel it when you walk around. It's time to clean this city up by getting guns out of the hands of children and off the streets, and let these spirits finally rest. With their help and your hard work, Gloomsbury can become a peaceful place. We can do this. We must send a message to law enforcement, to local government and to all the decision-makers in this city that the rampant distribution of ghost guns here is unacceptable. Halloween is coming up in a few weeks. Let's designate the night before Halloween as 'Ghost's Night.' On that night, take a white bed sheet and write the name of your loved one on it, then hang it from a window of your house. Let's bring these spirits alive and show this city how many lives ghost guns have destroyed." She paused and looked around at all the hopeful faces. *I'm doing this for them...*

She glanced at Lieutenant Vance, who put his hands up in a "T" as he nodded to her.

"I know it's wonderful to be here together, but unfortunately, we cannot stay much longer. It isn't safe here. While our goal is to make it safe in the future, the realities of today dictate we cannot linger here for more time than the police have agreed to protect us. They set a limit of one-half hour, and I'm asking you all to go home now, peacefully, and take with you the knowledge that you are not alone in your grief. By our sheer numbers here, we are showing city leadership we want change and will no longer tolerate violence in the streets. Go home now, do a good deed for a neighbor or friend, and let's decorate this city with white on October 30th!"

She hoped the citizens would heed her words and leave. Police were guiding people to pre-arranged exits. The crowd was thinning out, but some people were still coming in through security gates.

"Will you look at that!" Sarah pointed through the crowd. The Common, usually a large patch of burnt-out grass, was now a blazing rainbow of color. Bright, colorful flowers were arranged in an enormous bouquet. Isabella continued directing people, even as the police urged families to make their way to the exit gates. Em and Sarah gazed with tear-filled eyes at the growing panorama taking shape. Briefly, Em recalled her first lesson about guns with Henry, in which she had collected flowers as part of the video game. But collecting flowers in a video game paled compared to what she now saw in reality. She could never have imagined where that journey would take her.

"Come, I'll introduce you to Isabella real quick." Sarah grabbed her arm and pulled her onto the path. It was now 3:30 pm and a line of people stood outside the barricades, hoping to be let in. Police were blocking them, saying the event was over.

"You go talk to Isabella. I need to see if these people can still come in." She let go of Sarah's hand and made her way over to Lieutenant Vance.

"Can we please have another 10 minutes?" she begged.

Vance turned toward the cash box. Looked at it. Looked back at Em. Chewed his gum. "Looks like you brought in quite a bit of cash. Tell you what... pay me another $400.00 and we'll let all these people who are currently in line through. Then we're closing down."

She stared at him, trying to decide what to do. *It was outrageous that he expected four hundred dollars for only ten more minutes.* A part of her wanted to throw the money in his face, but she looked back at the crowd and swallowed her anger. Based on the number of people in line, it would probably take fifteen more minutes to let everyone in and get them moved through. She was sure she had the money to cover it, though it still rankled her.

"Okay," she said. "But everyone who is in line now has time to enter and put down their flowers."

Vance turned to his deputy. "Put a man at the end of the line, and don't let anyone else in beyond that," he said. The deputy scurried off. Turning back to Em, Vance said, "Looks like your little vigil was successful."

Em heard the disdain in his voice.

"This is a clear issue. People here want it cleaned up. What will it take to get that done?"

"Seems to me you're talking to the wrong people. You need to talk to them." He pointed a block away to a group of boys and young men lounging in the street. "As long as they're out there, there will be no peace in this city. We can only do so much to protect the citizens." With that, he walked away.

Gang members, Em thought. *Did Vance know of her connection to Danny?* She walked back to the Common, where Sarah was watching Isabella create a floral masterpiece with the donated flowers.

"This is incredible, Isabella," Em said. "It's exactly what this city needs. Thank you so much for your help."

Isabella said, "Glad to help. Flowers are my thing. These flowers will die in a day or two. You can photograph them and have the memories, but they'll be dead. Just like the people they're meant to honor. I don't mean to be pessimistic, but I think you need to be aware of what you're up against. Street gangs have ruled here for years, and that won't change because of one rally. In fact, they may retaliate with more force now. I sure hope you're being careful."

"As careful as I can be," she said. "I just can't stand by and do nothing anymore. I look at all these young kids, and all I can see is my friend Libby, whose life was taken. It's wrong. It needs to change. And now we know we have enough people on our side who care enough to do something about it. Even after paying the police detail, we have money to put toward other ways to fight gun violence here. I can't stop now."

"If I were you, I'd be wary of those police officers. In Gloomsbury, money talks. If they think you have money, they may try to get more from you. Don't put too much trust in what they say. My husband's a city councilor, and the council is constantly at odds with the police. Or at least he is. The council gives a lot of money to the police department without seeing much in return. It's a big black hole."

"Well, the police came through today and allowed this to happen, and I'm grateful for that. But I can see our time is just about up now." She glanced over the entry gates and saw the police were now turning people away again. The event was ending. "Thank you for arranging all these flowers. I will photograph them, and the pictures will be in the paper and all over the city for the next few days. We'll keep the memory of this day alive!"

Thankfully, while Em and Isabella chatted, Sarah had counted out eight hundred dollars and put it into two envelopes. Em made her way back to the Lieutenant to pay him. It felt strange to pay the police detail in cash, almost like a drug deal, but that was what he had asked for. He took the envelopes, nodded to her, and walked off. Isabella's words still rang in her ears: *Don't put too much trust in what they say...*

14

That night, as she settled into bed with a feeling of satisfaction, Em thought of Libby. They had met as toddlers and had quickly become fast friends. So many memories. She recalled their shared love of books and reading. Closing her eyes, she drifted back in time...

At school, she and Libby had been reading and learning about the Underground Railroad. She was 10 years old, at Libby's house, along with her younger brother, Danny. All the adults were away, and the two girls were in charge of Danny.

Libby bubbled over with excitement. "I discovered something last night," she confided. "My parents told me about this when they saw me reading that book. Follow me!"

Grabbing a flashlight and knife from the kitchen, Libby sprinted up the stairs of her house and ran to the end of the hallway, dimly lit by several old-fashioned sconce lights mounted on the walls. Dark paneling covered the wall at the end of the hall. Libby reached up behind the sconce on the side wall and turned a small hidden knob. She heard a soft click, then inserted the knife into the seam on the edge of the paneling and turned to Em and Danny triumphantly. The wall slowly pivoted outwards. Em and Danny stared open-mouthed as Libby pulled the door open to reveal a narrow, dark stairway. She scampered up the steps, twirling to face them when she reached the top.

"My dad says no one ever comes up here anymore, but he claims our house was once used as a hideout."

"Wait!" said Em. "Are there mice up there? I'm scared of mice..."

Danny chimed in. "She's terrified of mice! You should've seen her last night! There was a mouse in the kitchen, and she was screamin' an' hollerin' all over the place!" He flapped his arms wildly in imitation. "Eeek! Eeek!"

Em glared at him. "Shut up!" she commanded.

"No mice," said Libby with a smile. "Just a really cool room I want you to see. Come look!"

Em climbed the stairs with Danny behind her. The room was tiny, and the walls were covered with the same paneling as the door below. Libby aimed the flashlight at another sconce mounted on the wall. Once again, she found a hidden knob, and turning it until it clicked, she opened a second hidden door.

"There's a short tunnel, and then a room back there!" She opened the door and disappeared into the space beyond. Em gasped. Behind her, at the top of the stairway, Danny whimpered. "Where'd she go?"

"Come on in," Libby cried out. Danny stood frozen in place. "Don' go in there, Em," he said.

Libby poked her head out. "What's the problem? It's amazing in there!" Danny turned and fled down the stairs. Em shook her head. He was her responsibility today; if he chose not to be up there with them, she had no choice but to follow him back down.

"I'll see it another time, when he's not with us," she mumbled to her friend.

She woke up in a cold sweat. Was that a dream, or did it really happen? Jumping out of bed, she ran to the doorway of her bedroom and peered down the hallway. The wall sconces were still there, just as she had seen in her dream. Em had specifically chosen to keep them when she renovated the house because she thought they added character. The paneled wall at the end looked solid. But somewhere in the dim recesses of her mind, the memory of Libby opening the wall/door lurked. She had forgotten that particular incident and now realized why. It happened the day Libby died. She now remembered every-thing with crystal clarity. Danny ran downstairs, wailing that he wanted to go home. So... they walked the few blocks back to her house. Danny ran inside while she and Libby played in the driveway. Libby asked her why she was so mean to Danny, and she said he was a wimp. He must've overheard her say that and gone to talk to Sean. And then...

***

She tossed and turned all night. There was a secret room up there, above her bedroom. She was sure of it. *Was anything in there?* She promised herself she would check it out in the morning, but when morning came, she couldn't bring herself to look. The house couldn't possibly be haunted, but she called Henry just in case.

Henry had left a message a few days ago, but she had been so busy planning the vigil that she hadn't bothered to return his call. She hoped he'd understand and be willing to help her now.

"Hi Em! I was wondering if you'd forgotten about me."

"I haven't forgotten and I'm not ignoring you. I've been busy, is all. In fact, I was planning to invite you, Cara, and Ron for dinner soon. In the meantime, I could use your help here at the house. Can you come by in the next few days? There's something I need to check out and I don't want to do it alone."

"Sounds interesting... I can come later today if that works."

Gratefully, she hung up the phone and called Sarah.

"Remember you told me you used to hear noises at night coming from this house? You wondered if kids were using the house for storage, and that might be why Danny wanted me out."

"Yeah, I remember. Haven't heard anything at all since you moved in. I'm sure grateful for that!"

"Well, you may be right about a storage room. Last night, I woke up in a panic from a dream. But it might have been a memory. I think there's a hidden room in the attic of this house. The day Libby died, she tried to show it to me, but we got interrupted. I need to go into the attic to investigate, but I'm scared to do it alone. My friend, Henry, is coming over this afternoon and I thought if you can be here too, we could go up together to look."

"I knew there was more to that house than meets the eye! A hidden room in the attic! Count me in," said Sarah. "This is better than any mystery book I could read!"

***

She had hoped to do this during daylight, but it was late in the afternoon when Henry arrived. The setting sun cast an eerie glow on the outside of the house. Inside, light radiating from the antique wall sconces in the second-floor hallway had that same yellowish hue. The wall at the end of the hallway looked solid, but Em knew it opened to a dark stairway. She closed her eyes, recalling what Libby had done to open the door. Em easily located the hidden knob behind the wall sconce. Turning it, she heard a soft click and glanced back at Henry and Sarah. "Here goes," she said, inserting the knife into the corner of the wall. The door opened easily. There was the stairway, just as she remembered. Flashlight in hand, she went in first, and gasped when she reached the landing. It was exactly the way she had pictured it in her dream. The sconce next to the paneled wall was a perfect decoy. No one would ever think something was behind it. But Libby had said there was a room.

She turned back to her friends, who slowly came up the stairs behind her. "There's no way this room's been closed off for the last fourteen years. There have been people in here for sure. Look… there's a little dust gathered, but nothing like it would be if it had sat empty all that time. People have been in and out of here quite a bit, I'd say."

Sarah and Henry watched in silence as she turned the knob and opened the hidden door. It seemed stuck at first, but yielded when she gave it a good tug. She pulled it open, pointing the light into the opening. Sure enough, there was a short tunnel, though it was hard to tell if there was anything beyond it. Em was visibly shaking and the wavering light from the flashlight made it worse.

"Want me to go first?" offered Henry.

"No, I need to do this," she said. She wasn't shaking from fear, she realized. It was the memory of her friend at ten years old. Libby, so full of life and vibrancy, so excited to show off something cool in her house. Libby, just a short while before being shot. Em now recalled every detail of that day. *If only she could travel back in time. But then, what would she have done differently?* Slowly, she entered the tunnel. It was roomier than she expected, and it didn't take long for her to get through it and into the larger room on the other side. She shined the light around and was stunned into silence. Henry followed close behind her, with Sarah bringing up the rear. All of them gaped at the room, lit by the glow of three small flashlights.

"Holy Crap!" whispered Henry, breaking the silence.

"So this is why Danny wants me out. It all makes sense now."

Sarah said, "All those nights when I heard voices comin' from this place. At least now I know I wasn't imagining it."

The room was directly above her bedroom and was exactly the same size, but with a slightly lower ceiling. There were two tables in the middle of the room, each holding about a half-dozen partially assembled plastic guns, and lining every wall were shelves filled with gun parts, all neatly labeled and organized.

"I'd say the ghost gun industry in Gloomsbury is having a supply chain issue!" said Henry. "You're sitting on a gold mine. This might be their entire storehouse. Without access to this, that business is at a standstill."

"So... what do we do?" whispered Em. "Should we call the police?" She thought of her interaction with Lieutenant Vance the day before, and hesitated.

Sarah echoed her feelings. "I'm not sure you want to go to the police right away. Remember what Isabella said."

"I have an idea," said Henry. "How about we rig this house up so it actually seems haunted, and then lure some of these kids in here? We have something they need. If they come in here, we could scare the living daylights out of them. That might be a more effective way of getting them to reform their ways."

Sarah was all over that. "I know some of the boys who hang with your brother. They often come into the ice cream shop. If you're at the shop when they are, Em, we can have a casual conversation and make it known you'll be away for a few days and the house will be empty. We can set a trap for them."

"I like that idea," said Em. "But I'm not sure it will help me get through to Danny."

"Baby steps, Em," Sarah reminded her. "Start small, with his minions. If they're running scared, Danny will approach you and you may get more of an opening with him. Bring down the soldiers first, and the King will follow."

"Henry, can you really do this? Can you make the house seem haunted?"

"I can do better than that. I can make it *be* haunted. Forget about seeming that way. Those boys will never want to set foot in here again."

"Oh... I love this!" said Sarah. "Henry, can you get this house ready by Halloween? That'll add to the spookiness of it all!"

15

Danny paced the floor in anger. Immediately after buying the house, Em had put in new locks, and his entire supply of guns and gun parts now sat in his sister's house with no way of recovering them. It had been several months since his team of boys had assembled a gun. No supplies meant no sales, and with no income, the future of his business was at risk. All he could do was watch as she proceeded with renovations. *What if she found the storage room?* Surely, she knew of it. If *he* remembered Libby showing them a secret room in the attic, she would too. It was one of his earliest childhood memories, and one that had earned him his current status. When he first got involved in this business, they were scrambling for a place to use as a storeroom, and he immediately thought of this house. After all, it was abandoned, and looked as if it would remain so for many years. It had worked out perfectly until now.

He had thought he could scare Em away by talking to her, and when that hadn't worked, he'd sent a few younger boys over to break some windows. That had failed to send a message, and now the entire city was involved because of her vigil. Even the police were protecting her. He had been surprised to see Lieutenant Vance at the vigil on the Town Common. *Had she bribed him?* Vance had been *his* primary protection. Until now, Vance had given him free rein to use whatever space he wanted for storage. In fact, Vance didn't want to know where he was storing things. He had made that very clear from the outset. Vance had told him, "You bring me the money each month, and I'll order the parts. I don't want to know any other details of your business." Danny liked that arrangement. It gave him the freedom to run things. Yet now that he couldn't get his gun parts, he didn't think Vance would be much help. In fact, he was sure Vance would simply tell him to deal with it.

He needed to get into that house and get his business moving again, or he would be out of a job. He had secured space in an abandoned warehouse in another part of the city. Security was an issue there, and he would need a guard posted 24/7, but he could handle that if he had the supplies.

"Find a way to get into that fucking house!" he told his lackeys. "I need all that stuff outta there! Watch her, track her schedule and figure out when she won't be there. It shouldn't be that hard!"

***

Two weeks later, two boys, Chris and Petie, sat in the ice cream store, lamenting the change in their boss's attitude. Neither of them were keen on trying to break into the house while someone was living there. It was too risky. They had been following Em closely, and she didn't have any set schedule. So far, they hadn't been able to come up with a plan. Until today... when, as luck would have it, Em entered the store and went straight to the register to talk with the owner. The two boys listened carefully, though if they had been paying attention, they might have realized it was impossible *not* to overhear the conversation.

"I can't wait until the night before Halloween," Em said. "I want to walk through the city and see if people will actually hang out sheets. It will be like people hanging up Christmas lights. I hope it will help build a sense of community."

"Maybe," said Sarah. "But don't count on it. People around here hunker down and stay out of sight around Halloween. You may not get a huge response."

"Does anything happen around here on Halloween night? Do kids go trick-or-treating?" Em asked.

Sarah shook her head. "Kids used to trick-or-treat, but no more. It's not safe. For a few years, they had a designated time from 5:00 to 6:00 pm, but that ended a few years ago after a little girl was shot. Police don't want to be bothered with it, so they've told families to keep their kids inside. Oh, there are a few teenagers out and about, causing mischief, but no trick-or-treaters. It can be a bit of a scary night."

"Well, I've made up my mind. It's creepy enough in that house on a normal night. I'm going to be away on Halloween night. Will you keep an eye on the house for me?"

"Sure, no problem," said Sarah.

"Here's a spare key if you need to get in there for any reason." She placed the key on the counter, then turned and walked out the door without looking at the two boys sitting at the table in the corner.

Sarah busied herself with cleaning up. She walked into the back room, briefly leaving the two boys alone in the shop. *Would they be stupid enough to take the bait?* When she returned to the room, she had her answer. The boys were gone—and so was the key. She shook her head. *How dumb can you be?*

A short time later, two other boys came into the shop, and Sarah noticed the key was once again on the counter.

Again, she shook her head and called Em. "Looks like phase one of our plan worked perfectly. I swear, these kids have mush for brains. They must have made a copy of the key, and now it's up to Henry to use his magic."

"I hope this works. In the meantime, we have to promote Angel's Night for the night before Halloween. Hopefully, there will be a lot of white sheets hung up on October 30th."

16

From The Gloomsbury Post Ghost

'Twas the night before Halloween. Did you see what I saw?

I walked through the city with a feeling of awe.
Over 1000 bedsheets, each one with a name
From windows they hung, and none were the same.
It looked like a ghost town, all shrouded in white.
So fitting, since ghost guns have caused this blight.
Ghost guns have long been a scourge in our city.
They've pulled us down, and that's a pity.
With those guns in our midst, there'll be more ghosts to come.
It's time to wake up! Our work isn't done!

*Gloomsbury Leadership, are you getting the message?
These guns are unregistered, but you know who is bringing them in, manufacturing them, and selling them.*

Why won't you stop it? This place will become a ghost town if you don't act. How many more souls need to be destroyed before you do something?

***

On Halloween morning, Em entered the office of the *Gloomsbury Post* with a spring in her step, still flying high from the experience of the previous night. The paper with her most recent article had hit the newsstands early, and she was already getting text messages from some of her most ardent followers. She was sure it would be a stellar day, especially with what she had planned for the evening. She couldn't wait to talk to Samuel.

"What do you think, Samuel?" she asked. "The leadership in this city has to pay attention now." Samuel looked at her with a mixture of compassion and pity. "What's wrong?" she asked.

"They're getting the message alright, and they don't like it. Unfortunately, they're taking it out on me. They don't want me publishing any more of your stuff about gun violence."

Em was flabbergasted. This felt like her last days at the *Post* in Washington all over again. "Who's 'they'?"

"Our investors. The people who back this paper and keep it running. Some of them are also prominent city leaders."

"So... does this mean I'm fired?"

"Well, technically, I can't fire you because you aren't being paid to write these articles. You can still work here writing about local businesses, but you can no longer do that ghost-writing thing."

Em blinked and looked at the floor. She didn't want Samuel to see the tears forming in her eyes. She had had such high hopes for the work she was doing. "Are you getting any specific threats? I don't want to put you in danger because of the work I'm doing."

Samuel shrugged. "Getting threats is part of journalism these days. I can handle it, but I also need to heed their warnings. As long as I stop publishing that stuff, I'll be fine. But you need to be careful. Some of these people won't respond well if you continue to push your agenda. To put it bluntly, some of them may resort to violence."

She sank into a chair and hung her head. "I can't quit now," she whispered. "Over a thousand residents in Gloomsbury have suffered from this. I can't back away."

"I'm sorry, Em. Truly I am. Things might change in the future, but for your own safety, you should stay away from this issue."

She glared at him. She was getting angry now.. "Is that something they teach you to say in newspaper-editing school? Because those are the exact same words my previous boss said to me. Whatever happened to freedom of the press?"

"A free press went away a long time ago, once people realized they could control the press with money. The press is never quite free. Even if I was independently wealthy and could let you print anything you wanted, I'm not sure I could withstand the death threats that would come from publishing controversial material. There are a lot of crazies out there, and sometimes we have to alter our behavior to avoid setting ourselves up as targets."

"Well, okay. I'll pause my public writing for a while. You shouldn't be at risk because of me. I have a list of followers with email addresses and can contact them myself. Thank you for all you've done for me. Last night's display wouldn't have happened without you."

Samuel nodded in acknowledgement. "You be careful out there, okay? I don't want to write up something involving you in a body bag."

If only he knew, she thought as she left the office. It was going to be an interesting night, to say the least.

***

Late in the evening of Halloween night, four teenage boys crept toward Em's house. Each of them carried four large, folded cardboard boxes. An enormous white sheet hung from a second-story window, LIBBY written on it in a rainbow of big block letters. The sheet fluttered in the breeze, giving the house an otherworldly appearance.

Billy, the youngest of the four, piped up. "My mom told me these white sheets on all the houses mean something. They represent people who died from guns. Someone named Libby once lived here. My baby sister's name is Libby. Maybe this isn't such a good idea."

"It's hangin' jus' below the room we want to get into," Petie said.

"Come on, you two. We have a job to do. Danny will kill us if we mess up. Besides, there ain't no windows in that room," said Chris. "It won't bother us."

"Still, it gives me the creeps. Look—it's wavin' around like there's a breeze, but I sure don't feel any wind down here. I wish it wasn't there," muttered Billy.

"Yeah, well, let's just get on with this and get outta here," said Rob. "We got a lotta stuff to move out."

"Wait!" said Petie. "What about the ice cream shop lady? She said she'd watch the house. What if she sees us and calls the cops?"

"Danny tol' us not to worry. The police won't come tonight. He's makin' sure of that," said Chris. "Let's just do it!"

Emboldened now, the boys approached the front door of the house. Chris slipped the key in the lock, and the door magically swung open with a loud groan. The boys jumped, but then there was silence. "This goin' to be easier than we thought," he whispered to his buddies.

The house was pitch black, and the boys inched forward. Once they were all inside, Petie switched on the flashlight on his phone. They scurried toward the stairs, wanting to get to the windowless attic before anyone might spot the light through the windows of the lower floors.

"Did you feel that?" Billy asked. "There's wind blowin' through this house for sure."

"I don't feel nothing except your imagination! Let's get on with this," answered Chris.

"Geez, can you all walk a little softer?" demanded Petie. Though the boys tried to tread quietly, every floorboard creaked and moaned. They reached the second floor and scurried down the hallway to the wall at the end. With practiced expertise, Chris found the hidden knob, turning it until the door clicked open. Leaving most of their boxes at the bottom of the stairway, they crept up the stairs, collectively breathing a sigh of relief when they reached the top.

"Who's there?" said a voice. The boys froze.

"Thought you said the house would be empty," whispered Billy.

"Who's there?" demanded the voice again.

"Sounds like a li'l girl," whispered Chris. "I didn't think anyone lived here besides that woman." The boys huddled together at the top of the attic stairs. The voice was coming from the room directly across from them... the room they needed to get into.

"We need to get outta here," whimpered Billy. He turned on his flashlight and ran down the stairway, only to find the door at the bottom had closed. He couldn't open it from the inside. "Hey, we locked in here," he cried.

"I thought I heard someone," said the voice again. "How dare you enter my house!"

All four boys now huddled at the base of the stairway, trying to push the door open. It wouldn't budge. They pressed harder against it and heard a rustling sound above them. Was the disembodied voice coming for them? Light shimmered at the top of the stairway, and when it stilled, a young girl draped in a white sheet glared down at them. A halo of light surrounded her.

"Turn off your flashlights!" she commanded. The boys immediately obeyed, and the image grew until the sheet draping her blocked the entire opening at the top of the stairs. LIBBY was clearly written across her chest, mirroring the letters on the banner outside.

"I have a message for your boss. This house, and everything in it, belongs to me, Libby, the Ghost of Gloomsbury. Tell him that. Tell him he can only get what he wants over my dead body!" She let out an eerie cackling laugh. "He'll understand. Give him that message, and never, ever, come here again. I promise you, if I see you anywhere near here, you will be sorry. Now go tell Danno!"

Libby raised her hand and the boys heard the unmistakable sound of a single gunshot as the light at the top of the stairway went out, plunging them into darkness. The door behind them swung open, spilling them into a heap in the hallway. Fumbling for their lights, the four boys struggled to untangle themselves from one another. They grabbed their boxes and scrambled down the stairs and out the door, racing as fast as they could away from the house, the girl's laughter chasing after them.

"What the hell was that?" asked Chris breathlessly. "That house is haunted for sure!"

They slowed to a walk as they passed the house next door. It was shrouded in darkness, but as they crept by, a light went on in an upstairs room. In the window, the owner of the ice cream shop looked directly at them and shook her head. Once again, the boys ran.

17

None of Danny's friends dared approach him. Before, he had been angry; now he was livid. After the boys had given him Libby's message from the failed attempt to recover the gun supplies, he had thrown a lamp at them, forcing them to flee from his house. The boys had sworn the house was haunted, but Danny knew better. His sister was playing mind games, and he had to fix this himself. She might still think he was a wimp, but she was about to learn otherwise. He would prove to her he was brave and strong. But to do that, he needed to know what frightened her. As he paced in his room, a plan grew in his mind. If she wanted a haunted house, he would give her a haunted house.

It was well after midnight when he approached the house, carrying a paper bag and a handwritten sign. The white banner with LIBBY on it flapped in the breeze. The sight of it made his stomach flutter a bit. A more self-aware person might have recognized it as a twinge of guilt or remorse, but Danny was anything but self-aware, and neither guilt nor remorse were in his vocabulary. He grabbed a few pebbles from the ground and tossed them at the second-story bedroom window, then hid in the bushes. His sister came to the window, peered outside, and closed the curtain. *So, she was there.* he thought. *She must have set a trap for the boys!* It was time for his next move.

He crept to the front door and placed his sign on the ground facing the house. In blood-red letters, it read: "LEAVE." He reached into the paper bag, withdrew five dead mice, and placed them next to the sign. He banged on the front door three times with a rock in his hand, then hid in the bushes and waited again.

The door opened, and his heart skipped a beat when he heard the voice.

"Hello Danny. I've been expecting you." He felt his skin crawl. He remembered that voice. *How was this possible?*

"Come show yourself! I know you're there. Come talk to me!"

From his vantage point in the bushes, he could see a sliver of light in the doorway. *Was there a person there?* He couldn't tell. He stepped forward and gasped. Ten-year-old Libby stood there, framed in the doorway, a beam of light shining down from above. He stood rooted to the grass. *What was happening?*

"I want to talk to Em," he faltered.

"Why? So you can scare her away? No, Danny. You can't talk to her. You need to talk to me. I told your friends you could get what you want over my dead body. But guess what? I'm already dead!" She let out a short, cackling laugh. "You can't kill me again, but I can haunt your thoughts. We're going to have a little talk."

He looked around. If he ran, it would only prove to his sister she was right. He *was* a wimp. No, he needed to stay here and face whatever this thing was. *Just trickery, Danno,* he reminded himself. *It's Em playin' mind games.*

Light shimmered around the girl as she spoke. It was impossible for him to look away. "It wasn't your fault. I know that. I can forgive you for shooting me. It was an accident, and you didn't understand what would happen. What I can't forgive is what you did after. You desecrated this house I grew up in and you capitalized on guns. Countless other deaths have occurred because of manufacturing and trade of ghost guns. Every day, you expose more kids to this, with more chance the same thing will happen to them. For that, you should be damned!" The light surrounding her blazed brighter, momentarily blinding him. He shielded his eyes, and when he looked again, her head was enormous, her eyes the size of quarters.

Though his knees were quaking, he summoned all his bravado. "I didn't mean to hurt you, but it was so easy. I pulled the trigger—bam, it was done! Later, Sean kept tellin' me it wasn't my fault. 'She was jus' in the wrong place at the wrong time,' he said to me. He tol' me no one could ever call me a wimp again, and suddenly, I felt powerful. The gun—it gave me an identity. I was somebody to be feared." He pulled himself up to his full height.

"How's that working out for you? How many others have you shot at without a care for their lives?"

He shrugged. "What's a life? Doesn't matter."

"How dare you say that! The little boy I knew would never have said that, never in a million years! He *cared* about people! He understood *all* lives were sacred. Somehow, after you pulled that trigger—after you saw what happened to me—you changed how you thought and buried that knowledge. My question to you now is: Is it gone forever? Can you remember what you once knew? Can you remember that you cared about me?"

Danny took a step back and shook his head. The light was impossibly bright. "I don't know!" he cried out. For an instant, he was once again five years old. He looked at the image in the doorway and remembered Libby. She was kind to him, often taking his side when they were with his sister. He *liked* her—and then she was gone. *What did he feel at the time? Sad? Confused?* But then, Sean told him to forget about it, that it wasn't his fault and there was nothing they could do about it.

"Listen, if anyone asks, you know nothing about no gun, you hear me? I mean NOTHING!" Danny stared wide-eyed at his brother and nodded. "This is our little secret," Sean continued. "I gonna get rid of the gun, and then we pretend like nothing happened. We simply saw someone running by, and Libby got shot." Danny nodded again. Just to be sure, Sean made him repeat what had happened.

"We was just playin' in the house and saw someone running down the street. I ran outside, a car went by and you tackled me. There was a loud noise and Libby was lyin' in the driveway. That's all I remember," he said.

"Good man!" said Sean. "Don' add anything else to that, okay?"

Libby's image blazed brighter and seemed to grow in size. "I ask again: Can you remember your life before? You are the only one who can answer that. That little boy is still there inside you. Someone should have told you this when you were five years old, but no one bothered with you. Maybe, if they had, you would have taken a different path in your life. There is still time for you to choose a different way now."

"What other way? This is my life! My business. I don' know anything else."

"You're smart, Danny. You were always smart, even as a young kid. People will help you. Your sister will help you if you give her the chance. But first, you need to see what you did. You cut my life short. *You* did that. Sean may be right—I was in the wrong place at the wrong time—but *you* pulled that trigger. And now, countless other children will continue to do the same if you keep selling these guns. You have the power to stop this here, in this city. Think of how many lives you might save if you do that." Danny kicked at the ground, feeling deflated.

"And one more thing. You are not a wimp! A wimp would have run from here as soon as I appeared. But you—you faced me and you faced your past. There isn't much in life scarier than that. No one can ever accuse you of being a wimp. You don't need a gun to prove it."

The shrunken feeling he had felt was lifting. Maybe she was right. Maybe he could change. He looked again at the doorway, and Libby was back to normal size. She looked like the 10-year-old girl he remembered. "I'm sorry," he whispered, wiping his eyes with his sleeve. "I really am. You didn't deserve to die that way. You was jus' a little girl."

"The way you can show me you're truly sorry is by stopping what you're doing. Stop selling guns. Work with your sister to get them off the streets. Make the world a better place, not a worse one. If you do that, then I will accept your apology."

Danny blinked, and she was gone. The light switched off, the door slammed shut, and suddenly all was quiet.

What just happened? Had he really had a conversation with Libby's ghost? Libby seemed more human to him than ever before. He had cut short her life. Sean was right about one thing—there was nothing they could do to change that. But maybe he could do things differently now. He looked up at the fluttering flag, then at the bedroom window. The house was dark, but he thought he saw a flutter of movement behind the curtain. Gathering up the sign and the dead mice, he trudged home, deep in thought.

***

Danny awoke the next morning, unsure whether he had dreamed about the house or really gone there. Did it matter? He scratched his head, trying to push thoughts of the night aside, but all morning, the house, and the image of Libby standing in the doorway, loomed large in his mind. Something had changed inside him. Part of him wanted to believe it was all a trick, yet Libby had looked *real*, and she had talked to him. *Was it possible the house was haunted?* Maybe if he went there during the daytime, he could get some answers.

Even in daylight, Libby's house felt eerie. Danny stared at the front door, remembering Libby's face and the words she'd spoken: *There is still time for you to choose a different way.* "Was there?" he wondered now. Libby's ghost wasn't the reason he was afraid to go into the house. He was more frightened by what he needed to admit to his sister. How would she react?

He knocked on the door, and when Em opened it, he was silent. Despite rehearsing what he wanted to say, nothing came out of his mouth. He stood in the doorway, looking down and fidgeting from one leg to the other.

Em, too, seemed flustered. She frowned at her brother, unsure whether to invite him in or slam the door shut in his face. They stood there awkwardly and then both spoke at the same time. "What..." began Em.

"I..." Danny faltered.

Em motioned for him to continue.

"I want to apologize," he began. "Las' night, I came here plannin' to scare you away. But something happened. I'm not sure what. Maybe it's the house, or maybe I jus' had a bad dream, but your friend Libby spoke to me like she was really here. She said a bunch of things that made me think." Em watched him silently. "There's a room in this house..." he continued.

"I know about the secret room, Danny."

"You do?" He scratched his head as she nodded.

"Well, it's a problem for me. You see, that's my supply chain."

"How does it work?"

"A shipment comes in every six months. The room is full right now, cuz one jus' came in a couple days before you bought the house. We put everything here first, then sort and distribute it to warehouses all over the city. Five different stash-es. That way, everythin's not in one place. But the whole thing got blocked right after you signed that agreement to buy the house. The locks got changed and I couldn't get in. Everything was stuck here. I take orders, assemble the guns and sell 'em. But I can't sell those guns if I can't get in here and get the parts. Which means I have no money coming in now, and no way to pay for the next shipment. I pay my supplier up front... if he don' get paid, no new shipment comes in and everyone is angry. That payment is due in two days. My contact is gonna be suspicious when I tell him I can't pay it. He's gonna wonder why."

As she listened to her brother, Em recalled the day she had first looked at the house and what Libby had said to her: *There is corruption here and you are the perfect person to uncover it.* "Who's your contact, Danny?" she asked softly.

Danny squirmed and looked away. "I not sure..." he stammered.

"Oh... I think you know. You're just afraid to tell me."

"Look, you go to the police, all that will happen is I get arrested and they'll just move the operation somewhere else. It won't solve the problem."

"How would they know to arrest you? Are the police involved, Danny?"

Again, Danny was at a loss for words. How could he explain this to his sister? She was a *journalist,* for Christ's sake! If this got leaked, he would likely end up in jail for a very long time—or worse. That much he was sure of.

"Who's your contact?" she repeated.

Danny shook his head. "I can't tell you. He'd kill me...."

"Who'd kill you?" she pressed.

"Stop!" He cried. "He don' know you're my sister, or where I keep things stashed. He don' know any of it. I give 'em the money and he gives me the supplies. That's the way he set it up. But now... now I have no money to give him, and he's gonna wonder what's wrong. He doesn't want the details. He'll tell me to handle it!"

"And if you can't?"

"I dunno what he'll do. If he asks me where things are located and I tell him, you'll get arrested for sure. The police will claim you knew that stuff was there when you bought the house. If you bring me into it, and they realize we're brother and sister, the whole operation will just get moved somewhere else and both of us will end up in jail."

Em could see Danny was rattled. Being confronted by Libby's ghost had somehow reformed him, but she needed to know how much. "You said you came to apologize. What does that mean to you?"

Danny hung his head. "Somethin' inside me changed when Libby talked to me. She asked if I could remember my life before. She said I was smart and people would help me if I could realize what I did was wrong and apologize for it. I liked Libby! I didn't mean for her to die! It was an accident, but I was the one who did it." He looked at Em now with tears in his eyes. "Libby said the way to show I'm truly sorry is to stop selling guns and work with you to get them off the streets. I want to do that, but I don't know how. Truth is, I don't know any other way to live. Maybe I am just a wimp."

Em continued to stare at her brother. "A wimp? No way! No self-respecting wimp would dare come here and apologize the way you just did. You showed a huge amount of courage. Now it's my turn to apologize. I remember calling you that because I was frustrated that I wasn't able to follow Libby into that room. But I was so wrong to make fun of you for that. I can see you are one of the bravest people I know. I'll take you on my team anytime."

Danny managed a wan smile. "You mean it? Like we can work together and be a family again?"

"I mean it, Danny. You said your next payment is due in two days. I have a couple of friends who may be able to help."

"You mean your white friends that helped you fix up the house? You sure you can trust them?"

"I trust them absolutely, Danny. They are like family to me; we look out for each other. I know they'll be able to help both of us."

"Okay, but I need a plan soon. Like I said, if I don' come up with the money, my contact is gonna be furious. I may have to leave town before this all breaks open. He's already getting suspicious because word is getting out that our supply is low. I don' know how much longer I can put off telling him I don't have access to the parts.

"Okay—let's plan to meet two days from now at the playground near our old house. Be there at 8:00 am and have stuff with you in case you need to go into hiding for a bit."

18

E m sat on Ron's porch with her friends. "Birds," she mused. "I don't hear them around my house. All I hear are gunshots, sirens, and drunken brawls on the street. It feels good to get away from there." Though the yard was small, there was so much greenery. The forest beyond looked boundless. "I'd forgotten what it's like out here. I like my house, but this is so much more... peaceful."

Cara snorted. "I should hope so. I can't believe you're living in a house with a stash of ghost gun supplies! How do you sleep at night, knowing what's right over your head?"

"I guess I just tune it out for now, but honestly, I'm scared."

"You should be. At the very least, Danny and his four teenage helpers know those supplies are there. If one of them talks about it, you could be arrested. Who knows what Danny will do, especially if he's desperate for money?"

"Henry's hologram of Libby genuinely spooked him. It's amazing how something that isn't real can trick the mind so completely. I watched his reaction and I don't think he'd do anything to anger Libby right now, even though he knows she wasn't truly there. Yesterday, he was like a different person. I'm scared, but I would say he's terrified. He's caught between the ire of the ghost of the girl he shot and the person above him in this gun manufacturing scheme. He told me he may have to go into hiding for a while."

"Do you have any idea who his contact is?" asked Ron.

"I'm not sure, but I'm willing to bet Lieutenant Vance has a hand in this. Isabella Higgins warned me to be wary of the police. Her husband is a city councilor and deals with the police regularly."

"The sale of certain ghost gun supplies is a federal crime. How about contacting the FBI?" he suggested.

"What, and have them raid my house? If they don't believe me, I could be arrested. After all—there is an illegal stash of gun parts in a house I now own." She stood up and started pacing. "What a mess! How do I get all that out of my house and keep it out of the hands of those who would try to sell it? The whole point of me moving to Gloomsbury was to fight the scourge of ghost guns there. How do I do that?"

Cara chimed in. "I'd say you're doing a pretty good job already. You've broken their supply chain, at least temporarily, and one of their key players may defect to the other side. You're on the right track in thinking about how you can involve Danny in this. If he really has changed, can you use that to your advantage?"

"Maybe…." She pondered what Cara said. "For all his bravado, he sounded scared and I wish I could protect him, but I'm not sure what I'm protecting him from. I don't know how much help he really wants from me. "

"I have an idea," said Henry. "It's a longshot, but it might work." They all looked at him expectantly. "Make him a job offer."

"A job offer?" asked Em. "Doing what? I have nothing to offer him."

"You don't, but Cara does."

Cara looked at Henry in surprise. "Me? What kind of job could I possibly offer him?"

"Er, well, actually, you would employ him, but he would work with me. You see, in addition to monitoring online gambling platforms, I've been developing a few video games, trying to come up with kids' games that could replace the current violent ones that dominate the market. We can't control the production of those games, but if we can offer kids a fun alternative, it might weaken the industry a bit. I can do coding and game development, but I need someone on the streets who interacts regularly with young people—especially teenagers—and can enroll them to be testers. I have several prototypes now and I need feedback. Maybe Danny could be my liaison, to get them tested on the streets."

"Henry, that's brilliant," Em exclaimed. "Danny has quite a following, and this could give him a new sense of purpose. Sarah said he's a product of his environment, and she wasn't sure he could change, but I think he can. He's desperate for money, but he also thrives on power and prestige. He needs to feel like he's doing something important."

"Wait a minute," said Cara, scratching her head. "Henry, are you saying I've been paying you to develop video games for kids? Because that's not exactly in your contract...."

Henry blinked and squirmed, giving Em a sideways glance. "You haven't been paying me to do this. It's a side project born out of the work I'm doing for you. We're trying to create awareness of the dangerous practices used in the online gambling industry, right?" Cara nodded. "Well, the connection between online gambling and gaming for teens is very close. I've been infiltrating many of these sites and I know who their target audience is. It's teenagers. Very malleable teenagers. And the games are getting more and more real."

"We're supposed to be fighting against these companies," Cara said with exasperation. "To stop the use of addictive technology—not to push new games on kids."

"But the technology is here to stay," Henry argued. "It's not going away. Why not use it to our advantage to promote positive traits instead of negative ones?"

"He has a point, you know," said Ron. "Maybe this is something we should explore. There's some federal support for this now. There are grants available through the 'Break the Cycle of Violence Act' for corporations working to change the culture around gun violence. Maybe a grant could fund this."

"Maybe," said Cara. "But that would take time to put in place, if we even get one, and it sounds like Danny needs help now. More than a job, he needs a place to hide."

"I may be able to help him with that, too," said Henry. "After all, I am a master at changing identities and disappearing."

"Are you sure you want to get involved in this?" asked Em. "He's a total stranger to you. Plus, if you help him hide, you could put yourself in danger. We don't know what resources his contact has, especially if that contact is in law enforcement."

"Danny's your brother, and he needs help," Henry said simply. Em stared at him. She didn't know how to respond. Henry was an enigma to her.

Henry seemed flustered. "What I mean is, you all here are like my family, and if one of your family needs help, then I'm all in."

"Okay," said Em slowly, still amazed that Henry could think of her brother as family. And that he thought she was family. "In the meantime, what do I do about the stash of gun supplies in my attic?"

"I have an idea about that as well," said Henry. "We need to involve Libby. After all, she is the Ghost of Gloomsbury, and the house has a reputation for being haunted. Let's use it to our advantage."

19

Em approached the park with trepidation. The conversation with her friends the day before had buoyed her up, and she'd felt she could handle anything. But now, she wasn't so sure. She turned to Henry.

"Danny may be suspicious of you at first. Just let me do the talking, okay?"

Henry nodded as they stepped into the clearing. Danny eyed them from the swing. Back and forth, back and forth he went, like a pendulum. Em took a seat on the empty swing next to him, while Henry stood off to Em's side.

"I see you brought company," Danny said.

"I told you I was going to talk to my friends. My friend Henry here wants to help you."

Danny spat on the ground. "Why? He doesn't even know me. I don' need help from some stranger right now."

"Danny, two days ago you said you would work with me to get guns off the streets. We talked about being a team. Henry is part of my team."

"Well, THIS is MY team." He made a bird call, and his four young friends materialized from behind the trees, surrounding the swing set. "You told me you'd come up with a plan. I owe my contact money. I usually pay him something every week, but I haven't given him anything for about a month. Yesterday, he asked me if I was on track to pay him the full balance in two weeks. He knows something isn't right. When I told him I wasn't sure, he threatened me. I need the money."

"You said you might disappear if you can't get the money. What if we help you hide for a bit?" asked Em.

"Problem is, I can't skip town and leave my guys here to take the heat. If he sees I'm gone, he's gonna come down hard on each of them. I can't do that to them. If I disappear, we all go together."

Henry blanched. He had been prepared to help Danny hide. But Danny plus four others? This could be a big problem.

"So..." Henry cut in, despite Em's earlier warning. "If I understand correctly, you want to go into hiding and take your four friends with you?"

"Unless you have a better idea," Danny said. "Bottom line is they know where those guns are. If they get questioned about it, I can't expect them to lie. Sooner or later, it'll come out that the guns are in your house. If you want to keep that quiet, we all need protection."

"Are they the only ones who know where those guns are?" Henry asked, motioning toward the four boys.

Danny nodded. "No one else. These guys retrieve the parts and then distribute them to other warehouses where they're assembled."

Henry shrugged. "I guess you'll all be coming with me then. At least for a little while, until we figure this out."

Em glared at Henry. "What are you-"

"Trust me," he snapped. "I know what I'm doing!" Turning to the boys, he said, "If you want to go into hiding, meet me back here in four hours. Bring whatever you need for a couple of days."

Danny stood up and motioned to his friends to follow him. As they disappeared into the surrounding woods, Danny turned back. "Me and my friends—we need to talk about this. Maybe we'll be here, or maybe we won't..."

Em whirled on Henry. "Are you crazy? I know you're a master at disappearing and hiding out, but where are you going to hide FIVE boys?"

"I'm not going to hide them," he said. "You are."

"I don't understand..."

"Think about it. Your house was part of the underground railroad. That room, the one with all the guns? It was built as a hideout. It's the ideal place for them to be."

"What the hell? You want them to stay in MY house? In the room with the guns? Are you completely mad?"

"It's perfect, Em. Can't you see? The room is big, and we can make them comfortable, at least for a little while. I'll rig up a monitor to watch over them, and with their fear of Libby, they won't dare stray out of line. And while they're up there, they can test out my new games. Once they see how much fun those are, they won't mind being up there for a few days, as long as they're fed."

"You really are nuts," she snorted. "So now, in addition to a collection of gun parts in my attic, I will have a group of five guys up there who've been involved in the sale of those guns, who I have to feed. How does this make sense?"

"It buys us time. No one will know they're there, and we can work on rigging the house to make it totally haunted. Not to brag, but it's a brilliant plan."

"It's the stupidest plan I ever heard of in my life."

"Well, do you have any better ideas?"

Em glowered at him.

"Go home and box up as many of the gun parts as possible," he said. "Wear gloves. You don't want your fingerprints on any of it. The more you can put away, the better. Move it out of the way so the boys will have some space to spread out. I'll be by shortly with some monitoring equipment. Remember... back in the day, that room was a hideout."

Four hours later, the five boys returned to the clearing, each
with a sleeping bag and backpack. One at a time, Henry snuck
them into Em's house through the back door. At first, they
were reluctant to enter, remembering how Libby had threatened them a few days earlier. But when he brought them into
the attic and they saw the computer and monitor, their eyes lit
up.

"Why don't you put out your sleeping bags, and get comfortable while I tell you how this works," said Henry. "This
computer isn't connected to the internet, but it allows you to
communicate with us downstairs in case you need anything.
You can also play a few games on it. In fact, I want you to use
it and let me know what you think of the games. It'll make the
time go by faster. It's important you all stay quiet here until we
figure out a better place for you to go. Once word gets out that
you're all missing, people outside may ask lots of questions.
I'm sure you have cell phones with you, but they won't work
in this house. Remember... you are in hiding. That means no
contact with the outside world until I say so. Are you all okay
with that?"

He looked around the room, making eye contact with each
of them in turn. They all nodded.

"We'll order some pizza for you," Henry said, glancing back
over his shoulder as he left the room. The boys were already
engrossed in the computer.

***

Sarah brought pillows to the attic and fluffed them up for the boys. "Listen up! I'm in the house right next door, and I can hear everything you say in here. I mean everything. If you cause one bit of trouble, I'm goin' direct to the police and they goin' to bust your asses. Remember—you're supposed to be in here hiding right now... so BEHAVE!" The boys were gathered around the monitor Henry had brought in, completely captivated. She wondered if they had heard a word she'd said. "Did you hear me?"

"We're buildin' a city," Petey yelled enthusiastically, still looking at the screen.

"And we can put in whatever we want," added Chris excitedly. "How about a zoo? I'll be the zookeeper..."

"I'm glad you're having fun, but please keep your voices down," said Sarah. "You're in hiding, right?"

Gingerly, Sarah made her way down the steep, narrow attic stairs and found Em and Henry in the kitchen.

"I sure hope you all know what you're doin'," she said. "I'm glad Henry will be stayin' here tonight, but still, I worry about them bein' up there with all those gun parts. Right now, they're playin' some computer game. They said they're buildin' a city. What if they get bored and decide they don' want to stay?"

"We can't force them to stay," said Henry. "We can only try to get them to see there are better ways of living than what they've been used to. They're playing an interactive video game. I'm hoping it will entertain them for quite a while."

"Well, I'm going home now, but if you need anything at all, jus' give me a holler."

"Thanks for loaning us the pillows, Sarah," said Em.

Sarah smiled and closed the kitchen door behind her.

Henry switched on a monitor on the kitchen counter so they could see and hear what the boys were doing.

Danny said, "We need to have some open space, like a playground for kids. Let's put that near the zoo. And how about some picnic tables over here?"

"What about housing? Is there enough space in this city to give each family a small house with a yard? I hate the idea of apartments."

"We have a limited area for housing, but what we could make this little open field here a shared yard and put a bunch of houses around it..."

Em and Henry watched in fascination as the five boys created their ideal city. "Well, it looks like you were right about one thing, Henry. This game may keep them occupied for a long time."

"That's the plan," said Henry. "I want them to use the game to recognize they have options in their life. These games I'm creating—they're designed to open their eyes to possibilities. Think about what might happen if we fed all the teenagers in the world this instead of the violent crap they see every day."

Em looked back at the monitor and saw the five boys glued to the screen. "You might just be on to something..." she mused. "But speaking of feeding them...."

"I told them I'd get some pizza," said Henry. "I'll do that while they're busy with the game. Hopefully, whoever Danny's contact is will make his presence known, and this will get resolved within a day."

20

Vance stood in the hallway outside his boss's office. He raised his hand to knock on the door, then hesitated, took a deep breath and shook his head to clear it. Once again, he lifted his hand and gingerly tapped the door. He was terrified of the news he had to break to his boss. Danno had disappeared, along with four of his closest sidekicks. They owed him money. No one could tell him where they'd gone. This business was lucrative for Vance, and even more lucrative for his supervisor. He wished he could relay the news with a phone call, but the man insisted he come in person each month to give a report.

What could he say? How could he admit he had no idea what had happened to last month's shipment? That he had been completely "hands-off" in managing the details? He could picture the man's eyes bulging and his fingers curling into fists. But no, the man wouldn't attack him directly. He'd farm it out to someone far more capable. Vance shivered. He had no choice but to confess he'd screwed up. Why hadn't he kept closer tabs on Danno? He had insisted Danno do all the dirty work, mistakenly thinking that what he didn't know couldn't hurt him. Now he was about to pay the price for that ignorance. He stood now in front of his boss, his hands held out, palms up.

"I got nothing for you this month. My man always pays me from the past month's sales, but he stiffed me. Up and vanished. And from what I can see, he made very few sales the past few months. Almost nothing this month. Typically, the boys on the street are busy all month distributing, but they tell me no new guns have come up for sale. I wonder if he's selling somewhere else and trying to hide it from me."

"Find him! And find those gun parts! For Christ's sake, we're talking thousands of dollars for that shipment!"

Vance clenched his fists. *Yeah... thousands of dollars that would have gone into your pocket.* "I can't find him! I told you... no one knows where he went."

"What about that woman who moved to the city recently? The one trying to block gun sales?"

"What about her?" Vance sputtered.

"She made some trouble for us with her vigil and her newspaper articles. Maybe she found out your man was involved in trafficking guns, and she took it upon herself to eliminate him."

Vance was taken aback. Emiline Jackson? Was she connected to this? He didn't think so... and yet it was the only lead he had.

"You have two days to find him," the Boss said. "After that..." he shrugged. "I can't protect you. Your job here depends on keeping this going. If you can't do that, we'll have to find a replacement who can."

When Vance returned to the police station, the clerk nervously handed him a folder, saying, "Um... you asked me to find a file in the archives for you. It took me a while 'cause the case was so long ago, but here it is."

Vance opened the folder. Inside was a report he had filed fourteen years ago, detailing the shooting of one Libby Lewis. There was also a report filed by his partner, Ernest Swift. Ernie.... he was a black man, senior to Vance by about a year, and had quit the department several months after Vance started working there. Vance wasn't sure why Ernie left, but at the time was glad to be rid of him. In Vance's eyes, Swift was a "by the book police officer" and a stickler for details. Privately, Vance thought of him as "Earnest Ernie."

Vance read Swift's report now. It was far more detailed than his own. One line stood out: *Both physical examination of the victim's body and subsequent questioning of the girl indicate a discrepancy in the account of the young man. The direction of the shots was most likely from the house, not a drive-by shooting from the street."* Vance removed the page, crumpled it into a ball, and threw it in the trash. A moment later, he retrieved it, shredded it into small pieces, and tossed it back into the trash can. Then he read his own report. *"No gun was found on the property. Fourteen-year-old male witness stated, 'A car sped by and whoever was in it must've fired the gun.' He also said he saw a man running down the street, dodging parked cars."*

Before returning the folder to the clerk to re-file, he glanced at it one more time. The three children were named: Sean Jackson, age 14, Emiline Jackson, age 10, and Daniel Jackson, age 5. He looked up, startled. *Danno was Emiline's brother?*

21

Early the next morning, Em rose and checked on the boys. From the kitchen, she could see they were sound asleep in the attic, the room dimly lit by the glow of the oversized computer monitor. Henry was curled up on the sofa in her living room. She left him a brief note. *"I'm going to visit my florist friend. I should be back within an hour. Keep an eye on the boys and give them breakfast. Sarah left a lot of goodies for them. Her banana fritters are amazing!"* She snuck out of the house quickly, hoping to get to Isabella's flower shop before it opened.

Em found Isabella in the shop arranging flowers for the day's sale. She knocked on the door and a surprised Isabella opened it. Isabella put a finger to her lips and stepped outside.

"Can we talk for a few minutes before you open up?" Em asked.

Isabella nodded and walked away from the shop. "It's safer if we talk out here." They walked in silence for a moment, circling behind some buildings near the shop.

"Tell me more about this city. I've been away far too long. I thought I knew all about the history of gun violence here, but now I see there's a lot more to learn."

Isabella looked at her sideways. "I can't tell you much more than you already know, but I can tell you my personal story. I lost my brother Leroy twelve years ago. Gang violence. He was a sweet kid, just got caught up with the wrong crowd. My husband, Charles, was Leroy's best friend. That's how we met." She blushed. "Charles could've gotten angry and channeled it into hatred. Truth be told, he did get angry, but he fought it a different way and got himself elected to the city council. He was the first and only elected black councilor. He's fighting gun violence with politics, but often it feels like a losing battle. Getting the police to do something has been Charles' mission, and so far it hasn't gone well. This city is so corrupt. Guns keep coming in illegally, and he knows the police are involved, but he can't prove it."

"Maybe I can help with that," said Em. "Would Charles meet with me?"

"Maybe. He has to be careful, though. People watch the city councilors all the time, so it has to be private, you know. Even you talkin' to me could be dangerous for him. I'll let him know you're here and see if he'll come out. He's in the back of the shop. You wait here, behind this shed, and stay out of sight. If he doesn't come out in five minutes, then just go home and I'll see if you can meet another time."

Em waited, and a moment later, a tall, lanky man approached, then motioned for her to walk with him away from the shop. He looked to be a little older than her brother, Sean.

"I'm Charles Higgins. Isabella says you want to talk to me. You've made quite a splash here with your *Ghost Post* and that vigil," he said.

"I guess so," she replied, a little self-consciously, thinking about what Samuel had revealed to her about his paper's financial backers. "*Prominent city leaders who didn't want him publishing any more stuff about gun violence*" was what she recalled him saying. "Though it feels more like a trickle than a splash. Most people here want something better, but I'm not sure better is possible, given the people who seem to run things around here. There's so much history I don't know about. What can you tell me about the sale of ghost guns in the city?"

"I know a shipment comes in every six months, and the police have ignored it for years," Charles replied. "They don't want to know about it. Every time I've pushed them to investigate this, they've blocked me—both the police and the head of the city council. They simply won't engage in any action having to do with ghost gun sales. I find it hard to believe, but it looks to me like law enforcement officials want these guns to keep coming into the city, and they want them marketed to kids."

"Why do you think that would be?" asked Em.

"The only reason I can think of is that someone is making lots of money off this operation," said Charles dejectedly.

"Exactly!" said Em. "Gunrunning like this is a huge money-making scheme, and to stop it, we need to figure out who's at the head of it."

"Whoa... wait a minute. Who's this 'we' you're talking about?"

Em looked straight at him. "Isabella said getting the police to do something about gun violence has been your mission. It's mine as well, and I can't do it alone. Will you join with me?"

"Maybe, but it depends how you want to fight it. You may not like the way I work. I may be too cautious for you."

"I want information. You say you know the police are involved, but it likely goes beyond them. The question is, how do we discover who's in charge of it all?"

"I'm not sure we can, and if we do too much digging, we could be at risk."

Em looked squarely at him. "It's definitely risky. But continuing to live in this city without some kind of resolution of this is risky for every resident, every day. That's why I'm looking into this. I used to be an investigative reporter for the *Post*. In fact, I may still have a connection there who could do some research for me. But I need a starting point. What do you know about Lieutenant Vance?"

With a sigh, Charles said, "They hired Vance about fourteen years ago, around the time ghost guns appeared in the city."

Something gnawed at the edge of Em's mind. Suddenly, she snapped to attention. "You said fourteen years ago, right?"

Charles nodded.

"That would have been when my friend Libby was shot." She squeezed her eyes closed. "I think Vance was one of the police officers who showed up that day." *Might he have recognized her when she met with him to get the permit for the vigil?* She didn't think so, but still.... She turned her attention back to Charles.

"I remember those days well," he was saying. "I was a teenager and suddenly, guns flooded our streets. Every kid wanted one, and with the established gangs in the different areas of the city, there was a ready market."

"My brother, Sean, told me the same thing. He said ghost guns were simple to get and were pushed on teenagers. If you had just a little money, you could get an unregistered gun."

"That's right," answered Charles.

"So, can we tie Vance's hiring to the birth of this industry here? Was he recommended by someone?"

"I'm not sure who did the actual hiring, but the city council must have approved him. They might have records of his application, though all that is locked in the police archives. I'm not sure how accessible it is. If I go digging around in there, people will want to know what I'm looking for."

"I'll ask my former colleague at the *Post* if he can find out about Vance's past—where he came from and whether he had any ties to Gloomsbury before working here. It's possible someone with a plan to grow this business needed an accomplice in the police department."

"I'll try to get into the police archives, but don't get your hopes up." Charles said. "Who knows how far back their records go? Give me your phone number and I'll text you if I find anything out."

They exchanged numbers, and he started back towards the shop, but she stopped him. "Wait!" she called out. "There's something else I need to tell you."

He paused and turned back. "Go ahead," he said.

Em hesitated. She knew she was taking a tremendous gamble by revealing this, but didn't see any other choice. Having those gun parts in her house was weighing on her. She needed help to get them out. "If you know a shipment of gun parts comes in every six months, that means you're tracking those shipments, right?" He nodded. "Are you aware there's been a drop in ghost gun sales during the past several months?"

"I am."

"Do you know why?"

"From what I've heard on the streets, someone hid the shipment away, and no one knows the location. Only a handful of boys usually handle those shipments, and they've been silent all month. Last night, I heard they disappeared."

"Who told you that?"

"I have connections. I can't tell you their names, but I trust the things they tell me."

Em bit her lip. "What if I told you I know where those gun parts are—and where the boys are hiding?"

"How—?"

She cut him off with a sly smile. "I, too, have connections here."

He took a step toward her and glared at her. "Listen, you are getting into something very dangerous here."

"We both are. That's why we need to team up. I believe these boys don't want to keep peddling guns... but they need a role model who can show them there are other options. Would you be willing to talk to them?"

Charles said, "Why do you think they'd listen to me? I'm a fourth-grade teacher and my young students barely give me any respect. Forget about me being a role model for teenagers. I'm the enemy in their eyes. First of all, I'm an adult, and they mistrust all adults. Second, I'm part of the city government, and all these kids want is lawlessness. They have no interest in what I have to say."

"Do you really believe that? Isabella said you were angry when your friend Leroy was shot, but you channeled that anger into something more productive. These boys... they're no different from you at that age. They just need someone to show them another way to be. Think about it, okay?"

"No promises," he said as he strode away from her. "And good luck to you if you really know where those gun parts are located. Keep it to yourself—and definitely don't go to the local police."

22

L ost in thought, Em drifted back to her house after meeting with Charles, wondering if she had told him too much. Had she been too trusting? Maybe, but somehow, those guns had to be removed from the house, and she didn't know who else to turn to. And maybe it was time to get help from another source as well. She pulled her phone from her pants pocket and texted Jonathan, her former colleague at the *Post*, to ask if they could talk.

A moment later, her phone lit up. "Em! Thought I'd never hear from you again! How're you doing? Have you moved out of town?"

"I have, and I'm keeping a low profile these days. I'm in a small city and have been doing some writing for a local paper. No competition for the *Post*, of course, but it's been educational for me. I've run into a snag, though, and wonder if you could help me with a little investigative work. Do you still have access to the archives?"

"I do, but I have to be careful what I look into. Management has been pretty heavy-handed and it can be challenging to check things out on my own. I have to justify most of what I'm searching for. What do you need to know?"

"This needs to be completely off the record. Is that okay with you?"

"Depends," he responded. "Give me a little more information and I'll let you know."

"I want to find out about one person in particular. Lieutenant Vance, of the Gloomsbury Police Department. He's been working there for about fourteen years. I need to find out who recommended him for the job and what his background was."

"That should be simple enough. I'll have to come up with a reason why I'm looking into him, but I'll think of something."

"Thanks, Jonathan. Call me as soon as you have some information. This is urgent."

She replaced her phone in her pocket as she rounded the corner of her street and saw a police car in front of her house. Her pulse quickened. Lieutenant Vance stood on her doorstep in animated conversation with Henry and Sarah.

"What's going on?" Em asked, as she approached them.

Vance turned to her. "I have a few questions for you, Ms. Jackson. I didn't realize you had company staying overnight at your house." He glared at Henry. Though he didn't say it, Em bristled at the implication: *What was a white man doing at the house of a black woman early in the morning?*

"Who I have at my house is my business, Officer. What can I do for you?"

He looked her up and down. "I'd like to talk to you in private, if that's okay."

"No, it's not. I want my friends, Henry and Sarah, to hear everything you have to say."

Vance shifted uncomfortably. She would be far easier to intimidate if he could get her alone, but he could see she wasn't going to budge on this. "Okay... I'm looking for someone, and this morning, it occurred to me you might know him."

Em looked at him questioningly.

"Is Danno Jackson your brother?"

Em struggled to keep her composure. "He is," she said, choosing her words carefully. "What kind of trouble has he gotten himself into now?"

Vance cleared his throat. "He's the subject of an intense investigation here, and he's disappeared. Do you know his whereabouts?"

She shook her head. "Danny and I don't talk much. I'm sorry I can't help you." She turned to go into the house.

"Really?" Vance asked with a smirk. "It sure seems odd that you come barreling into town, complaining about gun violence, when your brother has been at the center of the whole operation for a while. And suddenly, he's gone missing. A little suspicious, I might say..."

Em looked from Sarah to Henry to Vance. "Wait, are you telling me Danny was involved in selling guns?"

"You didn't know that?" asked Vance. "Seems like everyone else around here did."

"Including you?"

Vance pursed his lips. "As I said, we're in the middle of a sensitive investigation here. We were all set to move in on him, and now he's disappeared."

"A *sensitive* investigation," she murmured. "Yet, a moment ago, you said an *intense* investigation and everyone in town knew about it."

Motioning toward Sarah, she continued, "Since our gathering on the Common, I've talked to a lot of local people who have told me the police have ignored this problem of ghost gun sales for years. Fourteen years, to be exact." She paused and noticed Vance squirm. "You didn't seem too keen on me hosting that vigil last month. And now, I'm supposed to believe my brother has been under intense scrutiny for a while? Something isn't adding up here. If everyone in town knew he was at the center of this, as you say, why have you let it go on for so long?"

"We didn't want to pick him up before we had all the pieces in place," Vance muttered. Em could see him turning red. Inwardly, she smiled. He was digging himself into a hole. Maybe she could trap him into admitting his involvement and give Charles his proof. If only there was a way to record it.

She turned to Henry, hoping he would catch her drift and play along. "What would Libby think of all this?"

Henry gave her a questioning look. "Huh? Oh yeah. She wouldn't be happy... not happy at all."

"Libby?" asked Vance. "Who's that?"

She turned back to Vance. "Libby was a friend of mine who used to live in this house. Since you were so curious earlier about my houseguest, I'll tell you who he is. Henry is what you might call a ghostbuster. I hired him to help me purge the house of the spirit that seems to haunt it. Libby's spirit."

Vance smirked. "A haunted house and a *ghostbuster*? Now that's a first."

"I been telling you for years this house was haunted, but you didn't listen," said Sarah. "I made countless calls to the police about it and they always ignored my calls. So many nights, I heard voices coming from the attic. This house is haunted for sure."

"Henry, why don't you go inside and see if Libby would like to meet this gentleman?" Em asked. "Maybe in our sitting room?"

Henry blinked rapidly, and tilted his head to the side. Then he straightened up, turned, and ran inside. "I'll check with her," he called back.

Turning her attention back to Vance, Em said, "So far, Henry has found Libby Lewis' spirit is quite agitated. She can't rest until the corruption leading to the sale of ghost guns is driven from this city. You see, my little brother shot Libby when he was just five years old. I was there and witnessed it. Danny got hold of a ghost gun that my older brother bought on the streets. That day changed the lives of everyone in my family. So, yes, I know Danny has been involved with ghost gun trafficking. In fact, Libby talked to him a few days ago."

Vance stood with his mouth agape. "A *spirit* talked to him?"

"Yes. I'm not sure what she said to him, but whatever it was terrified him and he ran. That's all I know. Sorry, I can't help you any more than that."

As she turned to go inside, the unmistakable sound of a girl laughing emanated from the house. Henry appeared at the door. "I'm getting signs Libby wants to talk to the Police Officer."

Em raised her eyebrows and looked at Vance. "Henry has brought in a lot of high-tech equipment specifically designed to communicate with the world beyond. Would you care to come in and see for yourself?" She beckoned him into the house.

"What's this foolishness? I don't have time to talk to a ghost," he blustered.

"You came here to get information about Danny. I can't help you, but maybe our resident ghost can. After all, she was the last one to talk to him."

"She's waiting in the sitting room," Henry muttered to Em. "And she's pretty upset. But the technology won't work if he has a cell phone in there with him."

Em held out her hand to Vance. "Give me your phone."

"No way."

"Okay, then leave. This is the only way we can do this. I don't care if you don't talk to her."

With irritation, Vance passed his phone to Em. She handed it to Henry and then led Vance into the sitting room. Henry blinked wildly as he rapidly typed on his keyboard in the kitchen. He whispered to himself, "I wasn't quite ready for this, but here goes."

In the sitting room, an image of a young girl appeared on the wall. Vance stood by the door and watched in horror as the girl appeared to grow out of the wall, becoming more three-dimensional with each passing moment. In his mind's eye, he saw this same young girl lying motionless in a driveway.

He jumped when he heard a voice. "We have a problem here," the image said.

"Who the hell are you?"

"I AM LIBBY! The girl who lay on the driveway in a pool of blood while you did nothing. In the fourteen years since I died, guns made here, in this city, have killed hundreds of others. Yet the police have done nothing to stop it. I've cried and wailed in this house, hoping against hope that something would change, and it hasn't. This has to end!"

Vance covered his eyes with his hands as the image blazed brighter. "What do you want from me?" he cried out.

"I want the truth. Why do you keep turning a blind eye to this? Who benefits?"

"I don't know what you're talking about."

"That's a lie! You must know. Someone is profiting from this. Tell me who it is!"

"You're crazy," he exclaimed. He turned to open the door, only to find it locked. "What the hell? Let me out of here!"

"NO!" the image screamed. "I've waited fourteen years for this. I want answers."

"Okay, okay. You're right! There is someone who profits... but I can't tell you who it is. He'll kill me, for sure!"

"Really? So your life is more valuable than the lives of countless others who have died and will die because of this? More valuable than mine?"

As he looked around the room, Vance knew he was trapped and broke out in a cold sweat. He now knew why Danno had disappeared. Danno must have ratted him out and then gone into hiding. If Emiline Jackson knew of his involvement and went to the city council, the council would fire him in a heartbeat, and once that happened, he'd be on the run, not only from the Boss but also from his uncle. He could see no other way out. What choice did he have? Somehow, he had to bargain his way out of this room and then skip town, like Danno had. Unless... he could convince the Boss there was another way. Libby didn't scare him nearly as much as the thought of what his uncle might do to him. Uncle Rafael had a long reach. But Libby was the one who held him captive at the moment. He needed to buy some time to put his plan into action.

"I'll tell you who the driving force is behind this, on one condition."

"You dare to give me a condition? Why should I give you anything?"

"Because I have information you want and you're not a killer. Listen...you have no idea of the evil that lurks here in Gloomsbury. I do. Once I give you this information, a target will be on my back. Give me twenty-four hours to clear out of town before you move on this. Promise me that, and I will tell you who's involved."

"You have my word," said Libby. "Nothing will happen for the next twenty-four hours, as long as all the information you give me checks out."

"The mayor..." Vance began.

In the kitchen, Henry sat back and let the computer record Vance's statement. "Hand this to him as he leaves," he muttered to Em, giving her Vance's phone.

Vance spoke fervently for the next few minutes. When he finished, Libby's voice reassured him. "Remember, don't underestimate me. If you try to outmaneuver me, you will pay." With an eerie, cackling laugh, she vanished from the room as the door behind him swung open. He stumbled into the foyer, grabbed his phone from Em, and ran out of the house without looking back.

***

Em turned on Henry as soon as Vance had gone, "What the hell? Why are you giving him twenty-four hours?"

He smiled slyly. "I have ways to monitor him. Giving him time also gives us time to figure out the best plan forward with this information. I'm wondering if you should get out of the city for a bit. Might be safer if you go visit Cara and Ron for the day."

She stared at him. "Running away is the last thing I want to do right now. I started all this. I'm responsible for whatever happens."

"I didn't mean it that way," he stammered. "You are incredibly capable. But you'll be a target here. Vance could decide to come back to arrest you. And you're no good to anyone if you're in jail. Go to Cara and Ron's. This is a tremendous story, and they can help you figure out what to do with it. I'll update Sarah on all this, and one of us will contact you if there are any issues here."

She thought for a moment. Maybe Henry was right. If Vance arrested her, even if he had no grounds, that would mess up their plans. Vance had given them a lot of information, and she needed to sort it out quickly. Cara and Ron's house might be the best place to do that. "You have a point," Em conceded. "I'll go there for the day and be back by sundown tonight. Make sure those boys stay safe upstairs."

"The boys are fine. They're keeping quite busy with the computer, and we're feeding them well. This will all be wrapped up by tomorrow morning."

***

She sat on Ron's porch, once again noticing the large gap between how people lived in the suburbs compared to her city. If only Gloomsbury could have some open spaces for people to enjoy.

"So, there you have it," she told Ron and Cara. "The lone police lieutenant in the city and the mayor have both been on the take for ghost guns for the past fourteen years. What the hell do we do with this information?"

Em's phone pinged. She pulled it out and stared at a text message from Charles. **"Thought you should know. I got into the police archives and found the file for the day Libby was shot. I think the file is missing some information. The log states that Vance and another officer, Ernest Swift, responded to the call. Both of them should have filed a report, but Swift's report is missing. I'm trying to locate Swift now."**

She looked up from her phone. "Vance may have tampered with the police report of Libby's shooting. That must be how he knew Danny was my brother."

"I can't believe you let that man walk away like that! He's going to come after you, for sure. Maybe you shouldn't go back there tonight," said Cara.

"I have to go back. I can't leave Henry to deal with this by himself. As for letting Vance walk away, what else could we have done? We couldn't hold him captive in the house. That would've been kidnapping. And since he is in charge of the police in the city, calling the police would have been useless. Clearly, we need to take this information to a higher authority, but I'm not sure who that higher authority would be in Gloomsbury. Plus, Henry assured me he could track Vance."

"How about going to the FBI?" asked Ron.

"I don't know. Remember, there is still a stash of gun parts hidden in that house, and now there are also five boys up there. The FBI could arrest me for that. What a mess! There is so much to sort out right now, and I don't know where to start."

23

Ernest Swift looked at the folder on his desk. This might be his lucky day, he thought. Two phone calls earlier that day, seemingly unrelated, had proven extremely interesting. The first was from an undercover reporter based in Washington looking for information relating to the hiring of Victor Vance of the Gloomsbury Police Department.

"I know you worked in Gloomsbury when Lieutenant Vance was hired, and I'm wondering if you know who recommended him for the job."

Swift had a general dislike of reporters and wasn't about to give out any information. "I know nothing," he said, ending the phone call. Out of curiosity, he checked on Lieutenant Vance's background. He had just started to peruse the material he'd collected when his phone buzzed again.

"Are you the same Ernest Swift who worked for the Gloomsbury Police Department fourteen years ago?" asked the caller, after identifying himself as Charles Higgins, a Gloomsbury city councilor.

Interesting. Swift thought. *Twice in one day*. He was guard-
ed in his response. His experience in Gloomsbury was one he
would rather not dwell on. "Yes, I worked there," he said.

Charles cleared his throat. "I know this is a longshot, but I'm
reviewing some old files and it seems there was a case in which
some paperwork from you is missing. I realize it was over a
decade ago, but I wonder if you might be able to fill in some
blanks for me."

Swift sat up. *Very interesting...* "I beg your pardon? I am,
and always have been, scrupulous about record-keeping. Are
you insinuating I was sloppy?" He kept meticulous records of
everything he filed, and had done so his entire professional life.

"No, no!" the caller assured him. "In fact, if anyone is to
blame, it would be the department itself and what it expected
of its officers. It's just..." the caller paused, "there was this one
case involving two officers, but only a single report was filed by
the other officer. I thought it was routine to have both officers
file separate reports."

"What is this case you are referring to?" asked Swift. He
wasn't going to admit yet that he kept copies of everything he'd
ever filed.

By the end of the conversation, Swift felt giddy with excitement. This might well be a breakthrough case for him. Tam-
pering with police records was illegal; however, he suspected
this went far deeper. He recalled his time as a police officer in

Gloomsbury, when he had naively thought he could make a difference in the quality of people's lives. He quickly learned the department had hired him as the token black man and he had no power to fix things. Still, a year into his tenure there, when they hired a new recruit, Victor Vance, to be his partner, he had hoped Vance would work with him to create some positive changes. Vance, though, treated him with disdain, and within a few months, Swift realized he and Victor Vance played by very different rules. Disillusioned, Swift had quit a few months later.

After that short stint in Gloomsbury, Swift had landed his current job with the FBI. Here, he worked diligently to bring law and order to what he thought of as an uncivilized world. The folder on his desk concerned Rafael Sterling, a man considered the father of the modern ghost gun, and one of the most dangerous men on the planet. Sterling sold kits made of 3-D-printed plastic gun parts, allowing people to assemble guns without registering them. The sale of gun parts was a hugely profitable business, but recent changes in laws required strict compliance. Swift was watching Sterling closely to make sure he followed the new laws, but he had missed a crucial piece of information until now—*Victor Vance was Rafael Sterling's nephew.*

If he had done more research into Sterling's earlier family life, he might have realized this sooner. But since Gloomsbury was such a tiny speck on the map, it had never occurred to him it would be such a lucrative market for Sterling's enterprise. Of course, he would use his nephew there! As Swift listened to the information from Charles Higgins and then read through the material he had collected, he suddenly understood Sterling's entire plan. The extent of corruption was astounding.

Years ago, Rafael Sterling had poured a large sum of money into the campaign fund of a prospective mayoral candidate in Gloomsbury. That candidate became mayor and remained mayor to this day. One of his first acts as mayor was to pressure the city council to hire Victor Vance as a police officer. Sterling then flooded the city with cheaply made guns, confident in the knowledge that his nephew would ensure the police would overlook this illegal activity. Swift now appreciated why his partner had been so quick to pass off the shooting of a young girl as the result of a random drive-by shooting sparked by feuding gangs. Gangs were the problem, not guns, and Vance had wanted the case to be closed out with little or no follow-up.

Based on what Charkes Higgins told him, Swift thought a lot of what was happening in Gloomsbury was illegal. It would be a major coup if he could take Sterling down over this. It was time to pay a visit to Gloomsbury. He wondered how much it had changed in the last fourteen years and how Victor Vance would react when he learned his former partner, a black man he had looked down on with scorn, was now an FBI agent.

24

He sat in his office, tapping his fingers on his gleaming mahogany desk. Layers, he thought. For years, he had kept his hands clean by having layers below him. Vance was one of those. But the layers were disintegrating. He had given Vance two days to find the missing gun parts, and so far, Vance had not done so. Vance was now a liability. He had to go, and the sooner, the better. But it had to appear random. He picked up his phone to place a call when an incoming call from Victor Vance appeared on his screen.

"Boss, it's me, Vance. We have a problem. That lady you told me to check out, Emiline Jackson? She knows way too much."

"What do you mean?"

"I discovered she's talked to my key contact on the street. He's disappeared and may have given her my name. I'm afraid she's going to do something splashy in the next day or so, and we need to cut her off before she does. Your reputation could be on the line."

"My reputation? How would your contact know of my involvement? This sounds more like your problem than mine."

"Yes... and no. I learned she used to be an investigative reporter for the *Post*. She has friends in high places and ways to uncover past information. It wouldn't be hard for her to tie me to you. She has to go. Tonight. It must look like an accident."

The Boss tapped his fingers on the desk with irritation once again. "You expect *me* to take care of this?" he asked.

"I was hoping you could help me out here. You have more connections than I do. Maybe a house fire?" Vance suggested. "The house is over 150 years old and in rough shape. I can pull some records and show she didn't do everything the building inspector recommended."

"The more people involved in this, the worse it could be for us. Did you at least get any information on that missing gun shipment? We're talking thousands of dollars of inventory here."

"Not yet, but I'm working on it. Isn't the timing odd? The shipment disappeared right around the time she moved in. She's behind this for sure, and I'm willing to bet she's behind the disappearance of my contact. We need to stop her now, before she learns any more. Once she's gone, we can turn our attention to finding the guns."

The Boss sat back, looking at his phone. He had been prepared to make a call to eliminate Vance, but this might be easier.

"Consider it done," he said.

***

Midnight. Against his better judgement, Vance hid across the street, peering into the darkness. He saw a flutter of movement, and barely detected a figure clad in black, emerging from the small copse of trees behind the house. The man slunk to the front door. Was he blocking the exit so no one could leave? Vance hadn't counted on that. *Makes sense to cover all bases,* he supposed. He shivered slightly from a combination of anticipation and a momentary twinge of guilt. He tamped down that feeling. *No room for guilt.* The woman was a liability, along with her friend. He saw a flash of metal as the man circled the house, sprinkling liquid from a small can. There was a brief flare of light from a match, then the unmistakable glow of a cigarette. Vance watched in fascination as the man tossed it toward the house. It landed a few feet away, and burst into flame. Slowly, the fire snaked toward the house. With a whoosh, the flames tore into the ancient wooden structure. By the light of the dancing fire, Vance saw the man melt away into the darkness.

Vance remained rooted to the ground, unable to tear his eyes from the burning building. He wanted to be sure no one escaped. It happened without warning; first a staccato of small blasts, like gunfire, then the popping sound of hundreds of bullets exploding. Brass casings spewed from the side of the house. *What the fuck? Was someone firing guns from there?* Before he had a chance to blink, the house was fully engulfed in flames. Moments later, the wail of fire trucks pierced the night.

***

Vance watched the house burn to the ground. No one questioned how he happened to be the first one there. In the chaos, most likely no one noticed. Finally, he went home and fell into bed, praying for a few hours of sleep before he had to return to the scene in the morning. *Why had he gone to witness it?* His mind kept replaying the moment the bullets exploded and the instant it dawned on him that the supply of guns was there, in that house, and had been there all along. He felt like an idiot for not realizing that earlier, but given his hands-off approach, how could he have known?

He should have been relieved. His problem was gone, along with her crazy ghost. She had to be gone. No one could have survived that inferno. Yet, as he was leaving the site a few short hours ago, he had heard a familiar laugh coming from the house next door—the house belonging to the owner of the ice cream shop. A laugh that sent chills down his spine. What about her ghost-buster friend? Had he stayed overnight at the house with her? Where were the bodies? Em and Henry had to have been in the house when it burned. He had seen them earlier that evening when Em returned to the house and Henry greeted her at the door. He had watched until the fire started and was sure no one had left.

After the fire, two bodies should have been recovered from the house, but no human remains had been found by the time Vance left the site. The forensic investigator said the explosions may have destroyed any chance of finding or identifying bodies. "It's still in the early stages," he had said, "but so far, nothing. Doesn't mean nothing's there, but proof of their demise might be impossible. I can't believe all the shell casings around here. Looks like a shooting range."

Vance trembled. That ghostbuster was a loose end he couldn't have dangling out there. And then, there was the neighbor, Sarah, who had run at him, pushing her way through the police barricade. Hysterical, she'd pounded her fist against his chest as he watched the house burn behind her. "You killed her," she raged. "I know you were behind this. This is all your fault. She told me about you, you bastard! The truth will come out and you will burn in hell!"

How much did she know? Had Em told her he was making money off the guns? It was certainly possible. Another loose thread that had to be tied up—or cut out. Vance realized he hadn't thought this plan through very well. In his panic, after revealing enough to Libby so she would release him, he had made a lot of assumptions. Now he had to be sure the woman and her friend were gone, and he had to go back to the site and make a public statement. He couldn't very well disappear this morning. The city had suffered an enormous tragedy (if you could call the destruction of an old eyesore of a building a tragedy) and it was up to him to spin it into a success story. A story of how that house had been used for the storage of ghost gun supplies, and now that those behind the distribution of illegal guns were gone, ordinary citizens could rest more easily. Yes, he definitely needed to put a positive spin on this. The mayor might not like it, but what choice did he have?

25

V ance approached the house with dread. He had to be there, but the memory of the previous night tormented him. *How much did Sarah really know?* As he neared the house, he saw her deep in conversation with several people. One of them was a Gloomsbury city councilor, but he had no idea who the others were. A woman stepped away from the group and approached him.

"Victor Vance?" she asked.

"Yes, I'm *Lieutenant* Victor Vance, of the Gloomsbury Police Department."

"Marilyn Greenly, FBI," she said, flashing her badge.

"FBI? What are you doing here? We didn't call the FBI in. This is my jurisdiction."

"No, you didn't call us. But we believe a major illegal gun smuggling operation was operating out of this house." She pointed to the rubble. "We're taking over full control of this investigation. I've already informed your forensic investigator, and he has turned everything over to us."

Victor's mouth went dry. "Gun smuggling?" he coughed. "That's ridiculous! You can't just come in here and take over!"

"We're talking about a federal crime, so yes, we can take over. Effective immediately, you are relieved from this case. We've interviewed quite a few people already and our investigation is taking shape. In fact, we have a few key people who will be here momentarily." She nodded to Sarah, who sent a text from her phone. A moment later, Danny emerged from Sarah's house, flanked by Petie, Chris, Rob, and Billy. Vance blanched as the boys approached.

"These boys have painted an interesting picture of how things have operated here for at least the past three years," said Marilyn. "They say a shipment comes in every three months and gets stored here before being distributed to several other small warehouses in the city. Were you aware of this?"

Vance stared at Danny with daggers in his eyes. "I did... I mean, I had no idea there were any guns stored in this house. Though, we've been investigating this for a while now." He pointed at Danny. "We were about to bring him in for questioning, but then he disappeared. You should know these investigations take time."

"Well, he tells a somewhat different story. According to him, the two of you had a financially lucrative relationship for a long time. Apparently, this house was sold a few months ago, right after they had stashed a full supply of gun parts in the attic, and recently, when he told you he couldn't pay you for this latest shipment because he couldn't get to the supply, you threatened him."

"That's a bunch of bull! I never talked to him in my life!" Vance yelled.

"You're telling me five boys regularly smuggled gun parts into your city, and you had no knowledge of it?"

"I told you, we were just about to break this case open!" Vance exploded. "We knew the guns were coming in, but we didn't know where they were putting them, or any other details. If anyone deserves to be arrested, it's *him*!" He once again pointed at Danny.

"We'll deal with him in good time. But that's no longer your concern. Victor Vance, you are under arrest."

"For what?"

"Illegal removal of police records, for starters," Agent Swift said, approaching the group, along with city councilor Charles Higgins. "Do you remember me, Lieutenant Vance?"

Vance peered at him. "Ernie? My partner from way back? You're FBI?" he sputtered.

"The one and only. Been with the agency going on twelve years now. It seems you removed a page from a file regarding the shooting of Libby Lewis. The police log showed that you and I were on that call together, but only your report was in the file. It so happened that this gentleman here, city councilor

Charles Higgins, was looking at that file, and noticed my report was missing. Mr. Higgins tracked me down, and luckily, I keep backup copies of everything I've ever filed with the police. My report is quite different from yours, wouldn't you say?" He showed the paper to Vance, who shoved it away.

"You can't arrest me for that. How can you prove I had anything to do with it?"

"Well, you're right... we don't have direct proof you were the one who removed my report. But we have a statement from your clerk. He says he gave you the file a week ago, and there were two reports in there at that time. An interesting coincidence, wouldn't you say?"

Vance fidgeted as his gaze shifted from Sarah to Danny to Charles to Swift.

"You are right," sighed Marilyn. "Illegal removal of police records might not be enough grounds for arrest, but when you combine it with conspiracy to commit murder..." She nodded to Sarah, who sent another text. Henry and Em stepped out of Sarah's house together and walked toward them. Vance blinked rapidly as Henry pulled out his phone and held it up. "We have an interesting recording. Half a phone conversation is almost as good as the whole one, don't you think?"

Henry pressed a button on his phone, and Vance's voice was clearly heard.

"She has to go. Tonight. It must look like an accident." There was a long pause. *"I was hoping you could help me out here. After all, you have more connections than I do. Maybe a house fire? The house is over 150 years old and in rough shape. I can pull some records and show she didn't do everything the building inspector suggested."*

Vance stared at Henry and Em. "How the hell?! I saw you both in the house."

"So, you were here, watching? Did you help set the fire as well?"

"What? No! Of course not! I mean—"

"Ever hear of the Underground Railroad?" Henry asked. Vance looked at him blankly. "Quite a few houses in Glooms-bury had secret rooms where fugitive slaves could hide as they made their way north. There is a network of tunnels connecting some of these houses, allowing the slaves to move along their route hidden from view."

"But... how...?"

"How did we know of your plan? You may recall that yesterday you gave me your phone for a short while. I didn't have time to hack into the phone, but I managed to attach a tiny tracker and recorder to the outside of it," said Henry. "Did you come back here to look for our bodies? For proof that the job was done?"

Vance's breath was coming in short spurts. He was trapped, and he knew it.

Agent Swift faced him. "Who are you more worried about, Victor? Your boss, the mayor of this city? Or your uncle, who helped get that mayor elected in return for his assistance in getting you a job. Which one scares you more?"

Victor's lip trembled, though he struggled to stop it.

"It doesn't matter much now because you'll all likely be going to prison. You see, Victor, these investigations take time, and we've been watching all of you for a *very* long time."

26

Danny sat with Charles Higgins in the fourth-grade classroom of the elementary school. "Your sister has gotten you out of an enormous heap of trouble," Charles said. "You understand that, right?"

Danny nodded and shifted uncomfortably. He looked at the posters on the walls to avoid eye contact. Charles had decorated the room with an eye toward inclusivity. "This room sure looks different from when I was in fourth grade," he said, pointing to a picture of boys and girls of many nationalities and races holding hands.

"Yeah, well, I want to make everyone here feel comfortable. We have so many rival gangs in Gloomsbury, and I'm trying to get these kids to see the things they have in common rather than their differences."

Danny nodded again. He was well aware of the turf wars in the city. He also knew that by fourth grade, many kids had already formed opinions of each other and joined gangs, often influenced by older siblings or neighbors.

"When I was a teenager," Charles continued, "street gangs terrorized many neighborhoods in this city. Rivalries often went back generations and had to do with different cultures. Adults passed their views down to their kids, and over time, these groups grew further and further apart. I have this crazy idea that maybe if kids from these rival groups can connect with each other before they become teenagers, then maybe they can build friendships instead of becoming enemies."

"Street gangs still rule. You really think you can make a difference?" asked Danny.

"I'm not sure, but I have to try. One thing I know, though, is that a gun in the hands of a teenager who is figuring out how to manage their emotions and where they belong in the world is a bad thing. Most kids have no idea how dangerous these guns are. They believe they are invincible." His eyes bored into Danny. "Your sister wants me to show you some other ways to live, but I can only do that if I know that's what you want."

Danny stared at the poster on the wall. "A few years ago, after I got busted for a minor robbery, Lieutenant Vance offered me a way out. I didn't want to go to jail, and he said he would wipe my record clean if I helped him with these gun shipments. It grew into a business I could succeed in. Other kids looked up to me and I felt like I didn't need to worry so much about the police anymore. Like, I could do almost anything I wanted and get away with it. Mostly, I felt powerful. But I see now how messed up that was." He looked straight at Charles. "Libby woke me up. I mean, I knew it was wrong to shoot her, but I always felt guns were a sign of power and never thought much about the damage they did. This life isn't for me anymore. I want to make this city better."

"Well, if you're willing to try, the City Council has a proposal for you. They are creating a special task force made up of local kids who will talk to other kids and come up with recommendations to make Gloomsbury safer. They want you and your four friends to be part of this."

"Do they really want our input?" asked Danny. "I have a hard time believing the adults here will listen to anything we have to say."

"You may be right, but if this city is going to heal, we have to start somewhere. I've been a city councilor for four years, and this is the first time I've seen a city-wide interest in change. Maybe they'll listen to your suggestions and maybe not, but if you don't try, you'll never know. This is a chance for you and your friends to do something positive for Gloomsbury. What have you got to lose?"

"I'll ask my friends if they'd like to help. Also, Henry offered me a job. He wants me to introduce kids to his new games and get some feedback. The game he showed us is called 'Build My Ideal City,' and we've started playing it. It's just a game, but in some ways, it could be real, too. Henry said he wants us to dream big."

"I'd love to see it. How about you get your friends together and show me?"

***

The five boys gathered in the conference room at City Hall to demonstrate the latest version of Henry's game to Charles.

"In this game, we're building our ideal city, and Henry told us to let our imagination run wild," said Danny proudly. "The first thing we had to do was give our city a name. We chose 'Libertyville,' in honor of Libby, the Gloomsbury ghost. She's the one who got us thinking about all this."

In the center of the screen, there was an image of a zoo, with a nearby playground ringed by picnic tables. A neat row of freshly painted houses stood off to one side. "Each of these houses will have two or maybe three families living in separate apartment units. We thought we could give them a shared yard space here. We want families to feel connected to each other but not living on top of one another."

"What about a central place for shops and restaurants?" Charles asked.

"We'll put that on the other side of the zoo," said Billy. "We also want to put in some public transportation so there won't be many cars. This is going to be a walking city!"

The boys had also added a school with an extensive sports complex nearby. "We need a teenage rec center," chimed in Petie. "It has to be someplace where kids can gather safely and blow off steam. The sports complex is good, but we need more. We thought of putting in a shooting range, where people can shoot guns legally. Only problem is, teens might not be allowed in there, unless we can work out some kind of deal with the police and turn it into a gun-safety education center, or something like that."

"I don't think kids in this city want all the gang violence," said Danny slowly. "Even the gang members might do things differently if they knew of a better way to live. Nobody has offered them any alternatives. A gun-safety education center is a great idea."

"Yeah, but where would the city get the money to build something like that?" asked Petie. "There's no way they'd do it."

"Well, I have some news for you about that," replied Charles. "You know all that money that you collected and passed on up to Lieutenant Vance for the sales of guns these past few years?" The boys nodded. "All that money went into the pockets of a few very corrupt people. The city council is suing the former mayor and several others for damages to the city. If we win these lawsuits, we may have a sizeable sum of money earmarked specifically to promote gun safety. The council will be looking for positive ways to use that money. They'll want to hear your ideas. I've been fighting for changes here for years, and I finally feel like things really can get better."

27

Lieutenant Vance stretched out on a bare cot in the county jail. The snoring of the drunk in the next cell had finally quieted, and he drifted off to sleep. Suddenly, he heard an all-too-familiar voice. "What have you learned?"

He sat bolt upright, looking at the four walls of his prison cell. She couldn't possibly be here, could she? He didn't see any physical sign of her, but the voice was unmistakable. He laid back down and curled himself into a ball.

"What have you learned?" she demanded again.

He sat up again and thought he saw a shimmering light. He spat at it. "Go away! You are nothing but a figment of my imagination. You want to blame someone, blame the mayor and my uncle. I was just doing what they told me to do."

"So you take no responsibility for any of the murders that have occurred during the past fourteen years while you were in charge of the security of Gloomsbury? Especially ghost gun-related murders?"

He shook his head. "How is it my fault? It's the culture of the city that's the problem. Gloomsbury loves guns. Ghost guns are cheap and easy to sell. I was just giving people what they wanted."

"And making a pretty penny out of the deal," she said. "Did it ever occur to you to try to change the culture of the city?"

"Why would I do that?" He spat at her again. "This city was doomed to failure from the start. It was a cesspool of crime when I started working here, and there was no way I could clean it up. That wasn't what they hired me to do."

Did she sigh, or did he imagine it? "I hoped you might change, but I can see you are not capable of that. May you rot in jail for the rest of your days." She let out a loud hiss, disappearing as the light faded away.

***

Danny woke in a cold sweat. Libby's voice echoed in his head. "What have you learned?"

He sat up in bed and buried his face in his hands. "Go away!" he cried out.

"I'll leave once my work is done. Tell me what you've learned," she demanded.

What *had* he learned? "That tunnel—" he began, "the one connecting those two houses. Neighbors built it to help each other out. They were working together to make the world a better place. If it wasn't for that tunnel, we might have died in that fire. Maybe I learned how important community is."

"What else?"

Danny closed his eyes and thought some more. "Seeing Lieutenant Vance and the mayor both arrested... I suppose I learned nobody is above the law. I used to think of myself as King in my little section of the city, like I could do anything I wanted and get away with it, but now I'm not so sure. Having a gun gave me power, or at least I thought it did. Em said fighting violence with violence doesn't work. No one wins in the end. I see that now. I don't need to sell guns anymore. Maybe you're right, and I can help make this city safer for kids."

In his mind's eye, he saw Libby smile. "I see great things in your future," she said as she faded away.

***

Em lay in bed in Sarah's guest room, staring outside at the gaping hole that had once been Libby's house. There was a rustling of curtains, and she heard Libby's voice, clear as a bell.

"Why are you so sad?"

"I'm sorry about your house. It's my fault it burned."

"That's not true! It's the price we had to pay to clean up this city. I know you will rebuild it and make it beautiful. And it will be your house, not mine. It's time for you to let me go."

"What do you mean?"

"I have to go. Thanks to you, my work here is done."

Em shook her head. "You can't leave! I thought you'd be around forever."

"Nothing lasts forever, though I will be eternally grateful to you for freeing me. I have to go, and you don't need me anymore. It's time for you to be yourself, without my interference."

"But I don't even know who I am without you. I've been writing under your name for years."

"Then you'll just have to re-invent yourself. Be a true journalist for the local paper. Be kind to yourself, plant flowers in your new yard, and always remember me."

Em was left with silence—silence in the room, and silence in her mind. Could this have been her last conversation with Libby? She'd gotten so used to having Libby around that she didn't realize the absurdity of it. Libby was the one she always turned to whenever she questioned anything. Libby was her alter-ego. She thought back to a question Henry had asked her long ago:

"Do you ever feel you are her? Or is it just that she speaks through you?"

She realized she had never quite answered that question. Libby simply coexisted inside of her, and Em had assumed that would never stop. Over time, she'd accepted Libby's presence, and it became part of her. Who was she without her ghost friend to guide her?

She fell back into a fitful sleep, only to be awakened by her phone several hours later. It was Jonathan, her former boss at the *Post*. He had left her a voice mail a few days earlier saying he had an interesting offer for her.

"Hi there. It's been a while," she said, struggling to sound as awake as possible.

"Hi Em. I hope I didn't wake you. I remember you used to get into work early, so I figured I'd take a chance and see if I could reach you. You haven't been great at returning my calls."

"Sorry. I've been busy. I didn't mean to be rude."

Jonathan cleared his throat. "Well, I have some news for you. There's been another shake-up at the *Post*. The current owners have reversed their thinking and want to re-hire some of their old staff. They specifically asked for you. I told them I wasn't sure what you were up to, but I'd find out."

Em looked at the phone. "Wait, you said they asked for me... did they mean me as Em, or Libby? Libby was the one they let go, right?"

"Actually, they want to re-hire Libby. It was a little awkward, because I didn't want to reveal your identity as Em, but I told them I would contact Libby's connection and we'd take it from there. What do you think of coming back here with the same arrangement as before? I'm willing to bet they'd give you a huge salary increase."

"No," said Em flatly.

"What?"

"I said no. Libby is no longer available. I've just accepted a full-time job writing for the local paper as Em and rather enjoying it. If they want to make me an offer to come back, I'd entertain the thought, but I no longer wish to write about fashion and restaurants. They'd have to allow me to write whatever I want, using my own name, with no interference. If they can't agree to that, I'm not interested." She knew as she spoke those words that the *Post* would never agree to it.

"You sure drive a hard bargain. I'll tell them, but don't get your hopes up."

"Jonathan, believe me when I say I no longer care what they think."

She clicked off her phone and looked around the room. Libby had said she was leaving, but Libby's presence couldn't be erased from this room so easily. Friendships didn't simply die like that. She turned on her laptop and starting writing:

Farewell to the Gloomsbury Post Ghost

The ghost gun industry here is dead, and Libby, the Gloomsbury Ghost, can finally rest in peace. I came here to be Libby's voice, but with her gone, it's time for me to be YOUR voice. Our community is safer now, thanks to all of you who stepped forward and let your voices be heard. We exposed massive corruption in our city and now need to rebuild trust in both the city government and the police. That will take hard work and can only happen if we come together as a community. Libby may no longer be watching over us, but I'm not going anywhere. I will stay as long as this city needs me. I have accepted a full-time position as a journalist for this paper, with the freedom to write about important local issues—even controversial ones. Stay tuned!

Welcome to Libertyville!

Did you hear the latest news? Our city is changing its name! From this day forward, this city will be officially known as Libertyville! A new name means a new beginning and an opportunity to create our city the way we want. Let's make Libertyville a model for peace and prosperity in the world.

Afterword

As part of my research for this book, I met with a former NRA certified instructor to learn how to use a gun. Standing at the shooting range, I considered the thousands of people who obtain guns illegally, and thus, miss out on this training. Too many of them are kids, especially those living in inner cities and towns where gang violence is rampant. Gun ownership should involve responsibilities, which are undermined when kids can easily get hold of guns.

In recent years, the number of guns has soared in U.S. schools. According to a *Washington Post* article in 2023 (1), over 1,150 guns were seized in K-12 campuses during the 2022-2023 school year before anyone fired them. That's over six guns each day, on average. Nationwide, 1 in 47 school-age children—1.1 million students—attended a school where at least one gun was found. Most campus gun seizures reported by news organizations involved high-schoolers—the median age was 16, according to the *Post's* survey. But authorities found guns on at least 31 students aged 10 or younger during the 2022-2023 academic year. *One of these children was just 4 years old.*

These numbers are staggering, but even more distressing is that it's likely local news outlets underestimate school gun seizures because of limited resources and efforts to keep incidents quiet. In certain communities, gun violence is so widespread that removing an unused gun from a school with children isn't considered newsworthy.

Unregulated, untraceable, and unserialized ghost guns are a major threat to our national security. From 2017 to 2022, the number of ghost guns recovered by law enforcement in the US increased from 1,600 to 19,000. That represents a 1000% increase. According to a report from the Sandy Hook Foundation, between 2019 and 2021 firearm deaths among U.S. children and teens rose by 50 percent, surpassing car accidents as the leading cause of death for these age groups.

While no studies have directly linked violent video games to violent behavior, a meta-analysis by the American Psychological Association found a connection between violent gaming and increased aggression, desensitization, and decreased empathy (2).

It is against this backdrop that I wrote this book. Given the ease of access that children have to deadly weapons, we are at a critical crossroads in our society. If we continue on this path, what message are we giving our children about how we view our fellow citizens and the value of individual lives? Is this the legacy we want to leave future generations?

References:

1. Klemko R, et al, "Guns are seized in U.S. schools each day. The numbers are soaring." *Washington Post,* October 10, 2023

2. Calvert SL, Appelbaum M, Dodge KA, Graham S, Nagayama Hall GC, Hamby S, et al. "The American Psychological Association Task Force assessment of violent video games: Science in the service of public interest." *American Psychologist.* 2017;72 (2):126–143

Acknowledgements

Many early readers gave me excellent feedback, and your contributions to this book were immense. Thank you to: Cam Finn, Esther Wikander, Carol Waite, Phyllis Bronson, Regina Walter, Joanne Hyatt and Joan Wright. I especially want to thank Rick Cooper, who gave me an enlightening lesson on gun handling at a shooting range. That experience helped me to crystalize the message I wanted to convey in the book. For writing support, I can't say enough great things about Karen Salemi, my incredibly astute editor. You have an amazing ability to see the holes and help me find clearer ways to communicate. I also wish to acknowledge Bonnie Heines for her excellent proofreading skills. Artificial Intelligence may be available, but nothing can replace the eye of a truly gifted proofreader. Of course, my most heartfelt appreciation goes to my husband, David Penfield, who read my very first draft and didn't hesitate to critique and ask questions. Your support of my writing means the world to me.

About the Author

Becky has a PhD in Biochemistry from Boston University, and worked as a research scientist before raising two children and opening a Yoga studio which she ran for 15 years. In 2018, Becky retired from teaching yoga to write full time. She considers herself a writer of contemporary fiction, and writes about the things that keep her up at night. Her first book, "When North Becomes South" was published in July 2020, followed by "Trapped in Pairadice," published in July 2022. "Ghosts" is Becky's third novel.